MW01268216

M-o-t-h-e-r Spells Murder taken as I was by the well... intrigue. Scheming mothers beware—Boatner has your number.

—Jonathan Odell, author of *The View From Delphi* and the widely-acclaimed, *The Healing*

Boatner is a fresh new voice in crime fiction. Equally eloquent and chilling, *M-o-t-h-e-r* will haunt you long after you close the back cover.

—Jessie Chandler, author of the award-winning Shay O'Hanlon Caper Series

M-o-t-h-e-r Spells Murder is a brainiac's mystery, with intrigue and clues behind every oak-paneled door and inside every bundle of faded letters. E. B. Boatner writes with clarity of lives warped by secrets and surprising obsessions. The book is meticulously plotted, packed with imaginative details, and welling with human emotion. Relationships that took root in the past are today's tangled vines.

—Elizabeth Sims, award-winning author of the Lillian Byrd Mysteries, the Rita Farmer Mysteries, and contributing editor at *Writer's Digest Magazine*

E. B. Boatner has written a gem of a first novel. Part traditional "whodunit," but moving quickly into the more modern form of "whydunit," Boatner's characters virtually seethe with life. With wry humor and an ability to plunge us deep into the center of the story from the very first page, this twisty tale begs the reader to curl up by the fire—or the air-conditioner—early because once begun, you won't be able to put it down. E. B. Boatner is the new guy in town, and definitely a writer to watch.

—Ellen Hart, author of *Rest for the Weary*, number twenty in her Jane Lawless Series

In Boatner's debut crime novel, *M-o-t-h-e-r Spells Murder*, readers will find themselves on a journey full of deception, intrigue, and jagged twists. With a distinctive voice and an appealing sleuth, this clever tale of mystery and murder will keep you guessing until the very end.

–**Lori L. Lake**, author of The Gun Series
and of award-winning *Buyer's Remorse*

With *M-o-t-h-e-r Spells Murder* E. B. Boatner serves notice that there is an exciting new mystery writer emerging onto the field. From a shocking murder at the outset of the story to the gruesome realization that actions from the past once thought forgotten or forgiven can most definitely spell violence, vengeance, and murder, Boatner reminds us there are monsters in this world. Warning: lock the doors and check under the bed before reading.

–**Anthony Bidulka**, author of the
acclaimed Russell Quant Series

I loved this book! It's the perfect sort of story to curl up with for a lazy afternoon by the fire, not so much WHOdunit as WHY? This wonderful novel reads like a PBS mystery. While it is clear early on who the culprit is, I was busy turning the pages to see how much vengeance he could wreak. And will the heroine Gwendolyn fall in love with the dashing police detective? What will become of the innocent British teenage boy? I raced through the final spellbinding chapters with the killer hiding under the same roof as his intended victims. I couldn't put it down and yet I didn't want it to end. Bravo! (Could there be a sequel?)

–**Mark Abramson** authors the noted Beach Reading Series

One Smart Why Dunnit. Set in 1980s New England, E. B. Boatner's first novel could have been written by a well-seasoned author with many tomes under his belt. In the first chapter of *M-o-t-h-e-r Spells Murder*, Boatner doesn't just dip his toes but plunges in with the savaging of seemingly innocuous senior-home resident, Elinor McGowan. Soon we find out who it was who killed her, but not why. We also discover that once upon a time, Elinor was the belle of her own ball and worthy of her own novel. The reader is fully engaged in this mystery along with the victim's wry daughter and the potential love interest police inspector, so the rest of the story involves watching them figure out and catch the murderer before he or she does someone else in—as will most certainly happen.

Like Ruth Rendell, E. B. Boatner has plumbed the depths of mankind's darker side to reveal generations past and how their corrosive relationships enable murder. If you like clever and cruel writing and fully drawn characters, I highly recommend *M-o-t-h-e-r Spells Murder*.

—**C.M. Harris,** author of *The Children of Mother Glory* and *Entering Oblivion*

M-O-T-H-E-R
SPELLS
MURDER

E. B. BOATNER

iUniverse, Inc.
Bloomington

M-o-t-h-e-r Spells Murder

iUniverse books may be ordered through booksellers or by contacting:

iUniverse
1663 Liberty Drive
Bloomington, IN 47403
www.iuniverse.com
1-800-Authors (1-800-288-4677)

Cover design by George Rodemer of G. Rodemer Assoc. (www.grodemer.com)

ISBN: 978-1-4759-4990-2 (sc)
ISBN: 978-1-4759-4991-9 (e)

Library of Congress Control Number: 2012917305

Printed in the United States of America

iUniverse rev. date: 10/11/2012

M & B
B & M
Y'All

ACKNOWLEDGMENTS

I never knew if an "Acknowledgments" section was really important to a book. And then I wrote one—and can now say with certainty, it is. And so, my thanks to Jimmy who has encouraged me from the beginning; to Timothy who discerned a "glorious mess;" to the Salon, where C. M., Laura, and Jen read, pondered, and suggested; to Greg, a.k.a. R1, who reads (and buys) author friends' books; to Jan, who actually inquired from time to time, "How's your book coming along?" To Mark, who asked tactfully and not too often, "Written anything lately?" To those busy, published authors who took time from their own work to gamely read mine and pen words of praise: Mark Abramson, Anthony Bidulka, Jessie Chandler, C. M. Harris, Ellen Hart, Lori L. Lake, Jonathan Odell, Elizabeth Sims. To all those dear friends who listened patiently (or gave every evidence of doing so) as I made my moan and who nevertheless still remain friends. And especially to my parents: To be raised in the woods by Southerners is to be given the gift of unlimited story material. Collectively, you all have taught me, *it takes a village to write a book.*

The past is not dead. It isn't even past.
– William Faulkner

CHAPTER ONE

For once in her long and stormy life, Elinor Buell MacGowan made no demand and offered no complaint. She lay mute, sprawled face-up on the shabby green carpet. Her left leg was twisted awkwardly beneath her, its stocking bunched around the swollen ankle. Her plump right leg was bare, obscene, stubby toes pointing at a black patent leather pump standing smartly upright a yard away.

Her head had been wrenched sharply to the left, as though someone had forcibly gained her unwilling attention. Elinor's eyes were open wide in a look that might have been construed as pained disapproval had it not been obvious that she was quite dead.

While Death was no stranger here in Copley Court, stealing in occasionally in the dawn watches to claim an elderly victim, He was usually forestalled by alert personnel who diplomatically removed the failing resident to hospital or nursing home. Well-trained attendants cloaked the rare unexpected demise—the absent breakfaster, the dozer by the library fire who had slipped unnoticed into his final sleep. The little cold that swooped to the lungs, the nasty fall and the hip that failed to mend, these were well within the province of the keepers of Copley Court. Never, in the eighty-six years of the home's staid existence, had anyone ever been called to her eternal rest in the hairdresser's basement cubbyhole by a bullet behind the left ear and a throat and torso savaged by athletic chops and slashes.

But then, as those who knew her would have joined in heartfelt agreement, Elinor Buell MacGowan had never behaved in a fashion either ordinary or conducive to the comfort and convenience of others. In earliest childhood she recognized the chasm between herself and the rest of humankind, and from that moment had single-mindedly devoted her life to impressing upon others the vastness of that gulf.

Elinor had not been a popular child, and now, having exceeded her allotted threescore and ten, she had spent the final eighteen months of her twilight years garnering the collective resentment of the residents of Copley Court, time and proximity only serving to widen the distance between her and her beleaguered housemates.

In an unusually short time she had alienated her coresidents through repetitions of her three sole topics of conversation: her parents, Wendell Byrd and Eula Fay Blair, and their idyllic life in what, to hear Elinor tell it, was a paradisiacal antebellum Atlanta some time before the O'Haras bought Tara and brought the neighborhood down; her late husband, the sainted Jefferson Davis MacGowan, with whom in actuality she fought pitched battles daily for fifty-four years until he turned purple one morning and quit the field abruptly in midargument; and her only child, Gwendolyn Anne, a silent, reluctant visitor to the vast brick pile on Boston's posh Exeter Street, who appeared weekly to submit to her mother's painful elaborations on these themes. It was a thorn in the side of many that Elinor wore her unpopularity as a badge of honor rather than a cloak of shame.

Seeing herself in her present condition, Elinor would have been torn between outrage at the indignities being perpetrated upon her person by a squat detective and a shabby police photographer, her decided inferiors, and satisfaction that she was, as she should have been, the center of attention.

The stocky, dark-haired man crouching over the body turned to the photographer.

"Weird," he remarked. "Shot *and* slashed. Overkill for someone her age, wouldn't you say?" Without waiting for an answer, Detective Edward Albano reached for a black purse lying half-open beside the body. "Through with this?"

"Yeah. It's been printed, go ahead," muttered the photographer, rewinding his film. "This is about wrapped up. Where's your better half?"

"Thibodeau? Upstairs trying to round up a witness, for what that will be worth," said Albano, rummaging through the purse. "The mobile ones don't hang around after they chow down, and the others wouldn't have noticed if she'd been done in at the table."

The photographer stepped over Elinor and began to pack his gear. "Not as much blood as you'd expect. Still, pretty ugly."

"Mmm ... Probably shot her first. CW will know." Albano knelt and examined the mangled throat. "He really worked her over. Wasn't taking any chances. Wallet's still in her purse. Just a few dollars, but I expect she wouldn't carry around much in here."

There was a sound of heavy footsteps, and a giant form carrying a medical bag filled the doorway. "'lo, Albano," the figure said. "What have we got here? Murder in the geriatric set? Look like robbery? No? Jesus, why do they always hand me this stuff on Friday afternoon? I had tickets for the Sox."

Albano grunted and went about his business. He knew from past experience that Chief Medical Examiner Claude W. Stafford was making idle conversation, not expecting a response. Corpses, and the ways they became corpses, were his obsessions. Accidentally drowned or strewn about Boston in baggies, it was all the same to CW as long as he could ferret out the whens and hows; the whys he left to Homicide. CW opened his bag and bent down to the corpse of Elinor Buell MacGowan, deaf to the chatter of the living.

The Copley Court duty nurse clutched the phone receiver and prayed for someone—anyone—to answer, regretting her spur-of- the-moment decision to look for Mrs. Evans's lost scarf in the beauty parlor. What she had found there would haunt her dreams. Finally, a click on the line and, "Hello?"

"Miss MacGowan? This is Sheila Sweeney at Copley Court. I'm afraid … I'm afraid I have some bad news …" She thrust the phone away from her like something unclean into the waiting hand of the squat detective.

CHAPTER TWO

A phantom spectator, she watched the elderly couple scuttle like courting crabs around the crowded notions shop. At least one of them was courting. Mouthing soundless entreaties, gesticulating wildly, the plump, auburn-haired woman pursued her mate as rapidly as her age and the narrow confines of the aisles would permit without ever gaining ground. The tall, mustached gentleman, his face beaded with perspiration, panted to keep his distance, snatching at the counters, scattering pins and ribbons in his wake, on and on, around and around. With a sinking heart, she recognized her parents.

Time passed. She couldn't escape—there were no doors, or windows. The air grew heavy with trampled dust and the very walls constricted. Sagging shelves soared out of sight into a vaulted gloom of faded spools of thread, frayed ribbons, and boxes so blurred with time and dust that their edges were rounded and indistinct, eroded gravestones of dead inventory.

Her parents continued their futile efforts, the one to seize, the other to flee, remaining 180 degrees apart, as they had in life. She was reminded of the black-and-white Scottie-dog magnets she had as a child and how she liked to hold them back to back and watch the negative poles repel each other.

Suddenly, an unseen hand thrust her willy-nilly into the drama. She staggered in front of her father, barring his way and tipping the balance of power in favor of her mother. Paralyzed, fascinated, the two watched her move inexorably toward them.

The scene blacked out. In the darkness a deep voice intoned, "Jesus, Designated Hitter for the Universe."

Gwendolyn Anne MacGowan sat up in bed. Covered with sweat, she peeled off the damp, clinging sheets. With shock, but little sorrow, she remembered that her mother had died yesterday. No, more than died—she forced herself to be accurate—had been *butchered*.

Numbly, she had listened to the news telephoned from Copley Court, had driven mechanically downtown to the police station to answer their questions and then on to the morgue to identify the body. She followed the detectives—Albano, she thought one of them was called—into the chill, tiled room where a young attendant casually pulled out a long drawer and pulled back the occupant's sheet.

At the first shocking glimpse, Gwendolyn thought irrationally of the dead Stalin. As a child, she had seen his death heralded in huge tabloid headlines, and had thought it a pity that anyone should die so reviled by the world. At twelve, she had been ignorant of the scope of the man's atrocities, but she had sensed the tragedy and loss inherent in the fall of an enemy.

Gwendolyn had stood, composed, looking down upon her own. Viewed from the chin up, her mother looked almost normal. In fact, Elinor Buell MacGowan could hardly have looked paler in death than she had in life. Her turn-of-the-century Southern upbringing—to which she interminably alluded—had shielded her from all contact with the sun's staining rays, and she never ceased to remind her tanned tomboy daughter that her own soft white skin had never been sullied by so much as a freckle.

Now that white skin was stretched tight over her patrician cheekbones. Her face seemed somehow completed, perfected, her life now consummated and sealed forever from outsiders—and from her daughter. Gwendolyn reached out to brush back a lock of auburn hair from Elinor's cold brow. She felt a sudden perverse twinge of pride that her mother's refusal to admit the existence of age, or of anything else she did not like or understand, had kept her tinting her hair its original rich auburn to the very end. Gwendolyn's touch was reserved and gentle, like an archaeologist brushing earth off a rare bone fragment. She was not shown, nor did she ask to see, what lay beneath the sheet pulled tight under Elinor's chin.

Gwendolyn shook herself fully awake and glanced at the bedside clock. Only 5:30 … A gray, spiritless dawn was breaking onto a Saturday morning poised to unfold its own special bleakness. Less than twenty-four hours ago someone had stalked and killed her mother, and today she had to go over it all again with the detectives who had escorted her to the morgue. Gwendolyn eased out of bed and headed down to the kitchen.

Gwendolyn MacGowan was a lean woman in her late forties standing just under five foot eight. She wore her dark-brown hair, now lightly streaked with gray, in a short crop, and her deep-blue eyes were intelligent and guarded. An intensely private person, her reticence and reserve were often perceived as sharpness and sarcasm by chance acquaintances. Gwendolyn's innate introversion and social awkwardness had been the despair of Elinor, who, at the birth of her only daughter, had cherished visions of cotillions, coming-out parties, and the Junior League to secure more firmly her own social standing. These hopes had dwindled, dying finally the evening eighteen-year-old "Gwennie" had, after a heroic struggle, been press-ganged into her coming-out cotillion at the Holly Ball. It was a disastrous evening by all counts, after which Elinor relinquished her hopes for her daughter's bright future in Atlanta society.

After nearly thirty years in Boston, Gwendolyn spoke with just a faint trace of a Southern accent. College had been her ticket out of Atlanta's life of endless social events, and from the emotional morass that was the MacGowan home; she had determined as she held her acceptance letter in hand, never to set foot farther south than New York City. In twenty-seven years she had seldom broken her resolve. Once, some years ago, when her mother was thought to be terminally ill, and, more recently, coerced by Elinor's entreaties to "At least come down for appearance's sake," to Jefferson's lavish funeral two years ago.

Alas, she could not prevent the South from rising again to haunt her. Immediately after her husband's death, Elinor, in a bold frontal attack, declared herself "too devastated" to continue to live in the "beloved" home that she and Jefferson had "shared in harmony for so many years" and announced her intention to come to Boston to live with her adored only daughter.

Gwendolyn, a seasoned veteran of such trench warfare, had parried with a flanking maneuver, securing her mother a suite at Copley Court, and making it clear in terms even Elinor understood, though never accepted, that there would be no living together for the two of them.

"And I'd tell her that again," Gwendolyn murmured aloud as

she took her coffee out onto the broad flagstone patio behind the house. She had found herself in Atlanta once more after all, to help with the sale of the house and the packing of Elinor's furnishings to be sent to Boston. That completed, she had returned as quickly as possible to the sanctuary of her own home and business.

Like many non-career-minded young women of her time who also chose not to pursue a "Mrs." degree, Gwendolyn had drifted through numerous time-marking occupations, clerking in a used book store, waitressing, and dabbling in freelance photography. Eventually, she had chanced to work for an older man named Edwin Bryce in his North Cambridge art framing shop. When Bryce retired, he offered Gwendolyn an opportunity to buy the business. With Jefferson secretly cosigning the loan—Elinor would be furious if she knew, he warned her—Gwendolyn bought the shop. Over the years she had built what had been a modest establishment into a thriving business with a solid reputation for producing quality work. She had five full-time employees, one of whom was invaluable for her experience in paper repair and the restoration of artworks and photographs. In the past several years, Gwendolyn had used her own knowledge of photography to venture into the buying and selling of original photographs, and had amassed a sound nucleus of pieces by well-known photographers.

The shop had enabled Gwendolyn to buy her Jamaica Plain home ten years ago at a modest price, just steps ahead of the yuppie gentrificators who swarmed into the neighborhood on her heels. At first, she rented out the third floor, but now that the shop was firmly established, she preferred the luxury of her solitude to the extra income.

Gwendolyn lived simply, dressing almost exclusively in slacks, jerseys, and sweaters, seldom entertaining or going out. She had nearly married once, in her late twenties, but had had the good sense to realize in time that she was happiest living alone.

Elinor, granted only occasional visits for dinner or a birthday celebration, continued from her redoubt in Copley Court to argue long and hard for "just a little corner of your big ole place." Gwendolyn writhed with guilt but knew with dread certainty that any "little corner" ceded Elinor would just be the command post for her grand campaign. *Lebensraum* was a term Elinor understood instinctively—she would gobble down Poland and any other nations with unguarded frontiers. Once installed, she would expand exponentially, her knickknacks and baubles spreading like kudzu on a dying tree, her authority metastasizing until Gwendolyn's home and life became conquered territory.

Gwendolyn had had to deliver the ultimatum that she would sooner sell the house, before Elinor reluctantly retreated to Copley Court to regroup her forces. For eighteen months now, Elinor had sighed and hinted and complained for the duration of Gwendolyn's visits. "You can't talk to these people, Gwennie. It's not like being with family," or, "You must be lonely, rattling around in that big house." Gwendolyn gritted her teeth and valiantly held her ground as Elinor chipped away at her defenses, a besieged Moscow with no General Winter in sight. But now, sipping her coffee in the muggy August morning, Gwendolyn realized with mixed emotions that some other more malevolent force had vanquished her adversary. Gwendolyn felt unaccountably alone.

CHAPTER THREE

As Gwendolyn woke from her dream Saturday morning, Carroll Goslin slipped out of his brick townhouse in the Back Bay, heading down Newbury Street and across Arlington to the Boston Public Garden. The ghostly heads of tethered swan boats peered at him through the witches' brew rising off the pond. The leaden air promised another suffocating day. Violence would erupt as tempers rose with the thermometer, but Goslin already lived with a full complement of rage. He could hold no more. Heat, cold—he barely perceived the elements. He strode along the deserted paths through the Common toward the Park Street subway newsstand.

Had there been anyone to notice, the tall, gaunt figure would have seemed oddly dressed for August. A thick, black alpaca coat brushed his calves at each swinging stride, its raised collar obscuring the lower part of his face. A dark felt fedora, odd these days in any season, served to heighten the pallor of his face. His eyes were immense; a brown so deep that the pupils were invisible; moist, with a light both lustrous and shallow—like the eyes of a corpse that died crying.

Goslin picked his way through the stacks of recently delivered morning papers, probing under the top copy to select two untouched copies from each pile of local editions. He stacked them to one side and reached into the depths of his coat to retrieve a small leather change purse. He counted out the exact price of the papers, and, avoiding the dealer's outstretched hand, dropped the bills and coins onto a stack of *Boston Globe*s. He hefted his own papers, cradling them in his arms like an infant, and strode back the way he came.

Pausing on his doorstep, he looked around on both sides before unlocking the deadbolt. With a final backward glance, he stepped over the threshold into the gloom and reshot the bolt. Goslin's building was a narrow, four-story brownstone, cheerful and tidy on the outside after a recent sandblasting and refurbishing of the trim. Inside, it was still Henry James territory. The walls of the narrow entryway were papered in a dark maroon, which deepened as it flowed up the stairwell, rendered more somber by the remains of a lush floral pattern in the faded echo of a forgotten color. Ranks of dull, white balusters ascended to the floors above, capped by a rich ribbon of maple railing darkened almost to mahogany through decades of smoothing hands.

Goslin padded up the steep stairs, his eyes half-closed, feeling the familiar treads solid beneath his feet. He passed the living, dining, and sleeping levels, continuing on to the top floor, where he stopped before a locked door, the keyhole dimly illuminated by a clouded bull's-eye window above the landing. Shifting the papers to his left arm, he pulled out his key ring and fitted a small, antique key into the brass lock.

Goslin smiled as the door swung open; he breathed deeply of the familiar odor of newsprint and yellowing pulp paper.

The inclined mansard walls made the room seem smaller than it actually was. It was difficult, in fact, to judge its exact size, for it was considerably narrowed by the ranks of dark-green file cabinets ranged around its perimeter. Cardboard boxes tied with string were piled on top of the cabinets, sloping in with the pitch of the ceiling, overhanging precariously like the interior of a vast, half-completed pyramid.

From the apex of this pyramid hung a long, white cord that terminated in a conical green glass lampshade. Goslin flipped a wall switch to illuminate a massive oak table in a circle of golden light. Several leather-bound scrapbooks were piled on the left side of the table, beside jars of paste and a brown stoneware jug bristling with pens, pencils, and a large pair of shears.

He set the papers on the right-hand side of the desk, squaring their edges to its corner. He slipped out of his coat and worn brown corduroy jacket, hanging each carefully on brass hooks on the wall. He closed the door and turned the lock, rolled up his pinstriped shirtsleeves, and reached for the top paper.

The glass shade gave his face a greenish tinge, while the glow from the lamp illuminated his smooth, white hands, modeling the thick, blue veins crisscrossing their backs. The hands were large for his body, yet beautifully formed, their pale fingers flickering lightly over the front page of the morning *Globe* like anemones feeding on the ocean floor. They spread the paper flat and held the edges secure as Goslin scanned each article, then slowly turned, secured, and scanned the following page, until he found what he was seeking.

"Elderly Widow Brutally Slain," ran the headline over a blurred one-column photo of Elinor that must have been taken with a Polaroid at some Copley Court function. It gave no inkling of the woman, he thought with irritation, no inkling at all. "Savage butchery … no motive or suspect …" There followed a lengthy description of Elinor Buell MacGowan, wife of the late Jefferson Davis MacGowan, former society matron and patroness of the arts, and so forth and so on. "She is survived by a daughter, Gwendolyn Anne MacGowan, of Jamaica Plain."

Goslin's sharp intake of breath was loud in the airless room. So Elinor had even lied to him about the girl's whereabouts … He reached for a leather address book, thumbed it open to "M," and, despite his trembling fingers, printed in a neat, librarian's hand, "MacGowan, Gwendolyn Anne," under Elinor's Copley Court address. At the top of the page was an Atlanta listing for Elinor Buell and Jefferson Davis that had been marked out with heavy troughed lines. He would check with information as soon as he went downstairs. He kept no telephone in this room.

Goslin replaced the address book and pen and drew the shears out of the jar. Their jaws sliced greedily through the paper. He kept them oiled and sharpened, and it was a pleasure to use them. It was a great shame, he mused as he cut, that the picture didn't do Elinor justice. He could have provided one … He folded the paper, placed it on the floor to his left, then laid out the second paper and began to spread, smooth, and scan it.

There were four clippings in all. Rather a meager amount of coverage, he reflected, but then, one couldn't expect the world in general to share his absorbing interest in the late Mrs. MacGowan. He moved the clippings aside and took down a dark-green scrapbook from the top of the pile at the side of the desk.

He opened it and was at once drawn down deep into that drowning pool of the past, into page after page devoted to a single topic: Elinor Buell MacGowan. "Mrs. MacGowan Welcomes

Governor to Symphony Gala"; "MacGowan Home Open to Garden Tour"; "Elinor MacGowan to Head Charity Drive"; "Elinor MacGowan Greets French Ambassador." The articles were noteworthy to an observer only for their singularity of topic, and for the fact that any mention or photograph of Jefferson Davis MacGowan had been inked over or razored out. Goslin worked dreamily through the volume, page by page, before setting it back on the stack of identical scrapbooks.

He remained motionless for several minutes, his great, dark eyes focused on some far vision, before rousing himself and moving to a set of file drawers. Opening the top drawer, he removed a tissue-wrapped oblong and set it on the table, tearing away the tissue to reveal a scrapbook bound in dull black leather. His nostrils caught the tangy scent of new leather; he caressed its fine-grained calfskin, his fingers tracing the words embossed in gold on the cover: "Elinor Buell MacGowan." Under that were the numerals, "1913–1988."

Goslin drew a white handkerchief out of his shirt pocket and rubbed the book in slow circular motions like a groom stroking a favored mount, then opened the volume to its first virgin page.

CHAPTER FOUR

The detectives made two unsuccessful rounds through a labyrinth of one-way streets before finding Gwendolyn's driveway hidden behind a stand of thick, gray-skinned trees, which had led the neighborhood, and the home in particular, to be called Beech Hill. Recently resurrected from the pink vinyl shroud to which it had been consigned in the 1960s, its gingerbread restored and its fresh clapboards painted dark gray and trimmed in deep maroon and crimson, the huge house had settled back comfortably into its Victorian darkness and gloom. It was a striking piece of formal architecture, incongruous, in light of its owner.

They pulled into the gravel driveway, winding between the overshadowing trees, and curved around to the left of the house, braking to a stop in front of a carriage house–garage. Gwendolyn, resigned to the depressing task ahead, had been watching out the window and opened the door before they could knock.

'You're Detective Albano?" she said, motioning him into the front hall. "And … I'm afraid I've forgotten your name."

"Thibodeau, Miss MacGowan. Warren Thibodeau." He spoke

abruptly, economical rather than rude. Thibodeau was clearly the senior of the two, midfifties to Albano's early thirties, lean, dark, intense. Gwendolyn watched him making a mental inventory of everything he saw. Thibodeau's head barely turned, but he was obviously taking in the golden oak paneling and cherry-edged oak flooring in the hallway, and appraising the tall shelves of books visible in the room to their left.

Gwendolyn ushered the pair into the room. "I'll be right back. I'm heating some water for coffee. Have a seat." She turned abruptly and strode down the hall toward the kitchen.

The two remained standing. "They used oak like we use Formica," remarked Thibodeau, running his hand down the door casing. "Look at those bookshelves, Ed, and that floor. Must be acres of hardwood in this place. Did you notice the wainscoting in the hallway? They don't make it like that anymore. Beautiful."

"Can't say as I did," said Albano, groping for the meaning of the word wainscoting, "but you're right. The place must have cost her a bundle."

"Depends when she bought it. A few years ago you could pick one of these old dames up pretty cheap."

The room stretched before them, a good twenty by thirty feet. Thibodeau figured it had originally been the formal parlor or drawing room, and had been refitted as a substantial library-cum-living room. Bookshelves covered every inch of wall space not taken up by tall windows that rose nearly to the ceiling and framed a wide, green-tiled fireplace to the right of the doorway. Three windows angled to form a spacious bay facing out onto the shaded front lawn. A window seat was set into the bay, thick, deep-green cushions peeking between stacks of books, and illuminated by goose-necked lamps arching out on both sides of the window casings.

The far end of the room was a work area dominated by a paper-cluttered table and high-tech office chair, while the center of the "living" area was a large television and VCR unit facing a comfortable, worn couch and two straight-back chairs. Several bookshelves to one side were filled with neatly labeled videocassettes. The room shone in the patina of golden hardwood, but the furnishings, though well cared for, were sparse, the isolated comfort spots designed solely for their owner—an owner not given to entertaining guests.

Gwendolyn returned bearing a tray filled with cups and saucers, a pot of hot water, instant coffee, dry creamer, sugar, and a small dish of cookies. She fixed her own coffee, then, indicating the tray, added, "Help yourselves." She sank down onto the green velvet couch, leaving the men to fend for themselves.

Albano shoveled two heaping spoonfuls of coffee into a cup and dosed it heavily with sugar and dry creamer. He poured in hot water, stirring the mixture until it had achieved the consistency of thick cocoa, and sat down on the nearest of the two chairs and waited for Thibodeau to begin.

Gwendolyn twisted the silver band on her right ring finger, became aware of her nervous habit, stopped, and picked up her coffee. She took a sip and looked impatiently at Thibodeau, demanding as soon as he sat down, "Have you found out who killed my mother? Or why?"

"No, not yet, but ..." Thibodeau halted in midsentence. *But what?* he asked himself. *No covered it pretty thoroughly.* He shook his head and collected his thoughts. He might as well be direct. "No, Miss MacGowan, we don't know much more than we did yesterday. There were no signs of a break-in anywhere in the building, no one spotted a stranger, and nothing in the house was stolen or disturbed, as far as we can tell. The hairdresser's salon was right under the kitchen, and with the lunchtime racket, no one heard a shot. We know you were at your shop at the time of the murder," he continued. "Are you there every day?"

Gwendolyn tucked her knees under her and hitched back on the couch. "I go in in the mornings to get the mail and see if there are any problems. My employees handle the orders and sales. I usually eat lunch in the Square—that's Harvard Square—then do my errands or shopping and go home. I do the paperwork right over there," she said, nodding toward the desk.

"When did you usually visit your mother? How often did you see her?" Thibodeau asked the questions while Albano took rapid notes.

"I tried to make myself go over two or three times a week. It was very difficult …" Gwendolyn paused. "I never went there for meals, if I could help it. I preferred to go after supper, when she was about to go to bed. She was a little more mellow then, had less steam to be aggravating, and I could sometimes have a real conversation, feel I was some company for her while she drifted off to sleep."

"Do you know anyone who would want to kill her?"

"You've gathered by now that Mother wasn't popular," answered Gwendolyn, "but that was just one side of her. They had a wide social life in Atlanta, and Mother could sparkle with the best of them—when there was someone to sparkle for, or when she was going to get a write-up or her photo in the paper for a symphony ball.

"Basically, she was a social snob. She thought I'd be a diadem in her social crown, but I was a dud. I thought she'd finally be pleased when I was accepted at Radcliffe—basically, Harvard. Instead, she moved heaven and earth to try to get me to stay down

South, go to Millsaps, where she'd gone, and kept telling me I'd love her Pi Kappa Delta sorority—horror!

"My father, who was always ashamed of growing up poor in Mississippi, said he wouldn't pay if I did go there. I was dying to go to Radcliffe—and Boston—anyway, so that wasn't a problem. It was weird though—I'd have thought a *Harvard* connection would have given her huge bragging rights.

"But I'm rambling. What I'm trying to say is that she could be delightful when she wanted to be. Here, she had no reason to extend herself for what she called 'a bunch of old doddards.' She was rude and difficult, but so are a lot of the others. I can't imagine rudeness caused any of them to do what was done to her. Anyone who didn't like her could just avoid her. Why would even a thief kill her like that?"

"I don't know," Thibodeau conceded. "It was brutal, but with the mix of drugs some of these creeps are on, some pretty weird and ugly stuff goes on. Crazy doesn't need a reason."

"What will you do next?" she asked.

"We'll hope that something turns up in her room, or that someone suddenly remembers seeing a stranger in the building that day. But if it was just a random killing, it will be that much less likely that we'll find him."

Albano looked up from his notebook. "What about your mother's will? Are you the sole heir?"

"I've never read it, but yes, I believe I am. At least she hinted as much. She had a younger brother in Oregon, but they hadn't been on speaking terms for years, and he died just before she moved up here. Mother told me once that she had planned to leave him a couple of thousand, but that was more in the way of an insult than a gift."

Gwendolyn hesitated and began to twist her ring. "I'm sorry. This is all unpleasant to think about. Mother was very angry that my father left me a rather large sum of money when he died. She made it pretty clear that it all ought to have gone to her and then she could have left it to me herself. It had absolutely no effect on her finances. My father was quite well off from his importing business, and he left her the bulk of the money, but it riled her that he made me independent. Just as my dad predicted, she had been furious when she discovered he'd cosigned a loan for my store—even though I paid him back."

"You haven't actually seen the will?"

"No. She kept it with their family lawyer in Atlanta and never told me what she had done. She and my father both kept their affairs—perhaps I should say their business affairs—a deep, dark secret from me and from each other. Here." Gwendolyn picked up a small, three-ring notebook from the end table beside the couch and handed it to Albano. "The lawyer's name is Seth Willard. His address and phone are in my book if you'd like to copy them down."

"Can you tell us something about how your mother spent her time?" asked Thibodeau. "Did she go out much? Did she have any contacts outside the house?"

"Hard for me to tell. She'd alienated most of the others, so she didn't keep company with them. At first she went out a bit with Claire Reizer, a woman I hired to be a companion, but mother wasn't having that—called her 'common.' Claire lasted about two weeks. Basically, mother just wanted to be with me—more specifically, in my house. Once in a while I'd drop by and she'd be out—I learned from the staff that she did go out alone a few times a week—never said where, and was usually home by supper.

She was in good physical shape, and her mind was clear, so she could get about.

"I know she enjoyed the Garden and the Common and window-shopping on Newbury Street—they're all nearby. She loved pretty things. But she was always vague about where she actually went. I'd ask at first, but she'd set off on a tangent about how nobody in the house would go out with her, how they were all rude to her, and so on, until I stopped asking."

Thibodeau got up and began to walk around the room as he talked. "Did she ever mention meeting anyone? Someone not from Copley Court?"

"No, not to me, but she had a vested interest in my believing that she hadn't any friends or social life. She wanted to live here with me, and she wasn't about to let me see her having a good time or being at all independent. And she was, you know, really."

"Was what?" asked Albano, his pen poised over his notebook.

"She was independent, certainly for a woman of her age from the deep South," said Gwendolyn, a note of pride creeping into her voice. "More than she ever wanted my father to know, and more than I suspected until I got old enough to see the difference between what she was saying and what she was doing. She'd hang on my father's every word and depend on him for every little thing, but when she really wanted something, she'd move heaven and earth till she got it, and I mean taking things into her own hands, not just whining until she got her way.

"When I was a little kid, she was always talking about writing. Then suddenly—I must have been about seven or eight—she took some writing courses at Columbia. Applied, and when she was accepted, simply packed up and moved to New York City for a summer. Found an apartment and lived there alone, taking her courses and doing just as she pleased. It made my father wild, but he couldn't stop her.

"And she did more than dabble. She had one novel published— *The Ceremony of Innocence*—that was quite well received. Wrote it under the name Evelyn DuLac. I don't think … her Southern upbringing, you know … she thought it proper to use her own. She'd written most of a second one, when something happened. She never finished it. Simply stopped and never mentioned writing again."

"What was it?" Thibodeau prompted.

"I don't know. It was another one of those secrets. I must have been about ten or eleven by then, big enough to know something was wrong, but that was all. You have to understand that everything at our house was veiled. They might let out a name or an accusation now and then, but there was never anything really to get a grip on. My parents fought all the time, but it was ostensibly over something like my father feeding Mother's fresh bread to the birds instead of using a stale loaf. We weren't going hungry, so I knew that wasn't really what they were arguing about. You could just feel their rage, and even a kid knows that's not generated by bread crumbs."

"Our men went over her room pretty thoroughly, Miss MacGowan," said Thibodeau, "but they didn't find anything. We'd like to ask you to ride down there with us now. You might be able to spot something we missed, since you spent time there with your mother."

"All right."

Thibodeau had his back to her, looking over the titles in one of the bookshelves. "By the way," he said, still examining the spines of the books, "do you own a gun?"

"Several, as a matter of fact," said Gwendolyn, stacking the cups onto the tray. "Would you like to see them?"

CHAPTER FIVE

Albano threaded his way back to Centre Street and turned toward the Jamaicaway, grateful to be heading back to his own bailiwick. Thibodeau sat on the front seat beside him, lost in thought. He had been startled when Gwendolyn returned to the living room with a bulging canvas bag and a small hard-shell gun case to display a miscellany of small arms.

"This is my favorite," she'd said, picking up a Steyr 9mm automatic. "Takes eighteen rounds in the clip plus one in the chamber ... and I like this little one for every day." She lifted her shirt to show the butt of the tiny Freedom Arms revolver tucked in her watch pocket. "Holds five .22s, but I keep it on an empty chamber, so there's only four. Enough if you're accurate."

There hadn't been time to question her before they had to leave, but now Thibodeau half-turned to face Gwendolyn in the backseat. "So why the arsenal? You can't need all those for protection."

"No." She had to speak loudly to be heard over the noise of the engine. "I just like them. I took up shooting when Mother moved up here. It was a dramatic way to let off steam, I guess, but it worked. I joined a club, took their safety course, got my permit, and started shooting combat matches. Obviously, you've got to shoot the snubby matches with a snubby, and the automatic matches with an automatic, and so forth, so I began picking up different pieces. Besides, it's like any hobby. You get hooked and pretty soon you're buying more equipment."

"You a good shot?"

"Fair. I've gotten a few trophies at the lower levels, but I don't have the discipline and concentration to be consistently good. I go for the company as much as the competition. That and the fact that the club door is locked and no one who knows me has the phone number. Have you gone through her room yet?"

"Yes, pretty thoroughly." Thibodeau did not comment on her change of subject. "It was sealed off after the … after. Routine. Nothing to speak of, though—a number of books, old letters, cards, condolences for your father's death and so forth. Nothing looked like anyone else had been through it."

"They were both packrats. Neither one ever threw anything away. My garage is filled with stuff that I haven't been able to deal with. I tried once after Mother sold the house, and I'd shipped all their stuff up here and stored it. The thing out of the first box I opened was my grandmother's grade-school report cards—from the 1880s. I taped it back up and haven't opened another. People tell me I'm lucky to have all that history at my fingertips, but I feel like a scared kid in the dark who has real monsters under my bed."

Albano looped the car off the ramp onto Storrow Drive and took the first exit onto Clarendon Street. As luck would have it, a car was just pulling out of a legitimate parking space. Albano quickly maneuvered into it, and the three walked the short distance to Copley Court. As they entered the lobby, three elderly women and a wizened gentleman with a walker stopped talking and peered at them intently, rolling their eyes like spooked horses at these people so intimately involved in the violent death of one of their own.

Elinor's rooms were on the third floor, in a back corner overlooking an alley further obscured by a dense growth of ailanthus trees. In this section of Boston small alleyways ran between the main streets, clogged by delivery trucks and affording parking for a fortunate few. Copley Court had originally been a private home, one of many such in the area fallen on hard times just after the turn of the century and sold to developers who carved them into apartments. Sometime in the 1960s, this one had been further deconstructed into an assisted-living facility. Two elevators had been added at either end of the building, but the main staircase, the stained-glass windows in the library and the chandeliers in the entryway and dining room had been left intact.

Elinor's suite encompassed two rooms and a spacious bath. The living room was crammed with her favorite pieces of furniture and, like most of the larger rooms in the building, had a marble fireplace and high, wide windows.

Gwendolyn looked at Elinor's transplanted sofa and wingback armchairs, her spindle-legged tables laden with bits of ceramic and glass, her portraits and watercolors crowded on the walls, and realized with a pang that she had in her own home created a pale reflection of Elinor's prolific overdecoration. Elinor's excess had always irritated her, but she appreciated her mother's many fine pieces, and, with a less lavish hand, had appropriated a few cherished objects to place about her, an unconscious homage to her mother.

Another part of her, she now perceived, emulated her father. Her Charrette halogen lamps and the German mechanical pencils she accumulated, the possessiveness she felt about her own assortment of guns and books and video equipment, were not so different from her father's obsessions, when he swore that he needed another bespoke bamboo fly rod and that each one of his dozens of fountain pens served a special purpose. Ever since she left the Atlanta house, Gwendolyn had prided herself on her independence of thought and action, while in reality she had been fragmenting her life between Jefferson's and Elinor's worlds. Was what she had taken for free will simply a child's futile attempt to please her parents?

"Notice anything?" Thibodeau broke into her thoughts.

Gwendolyn glanced about the room briefly. "She has so many things, it's hard to tell if anything's been moved. This is only her Southern collection. I had to put a ton of her books in a real storage locker—my garage isn't big enough—but these were her special pride and joy. She was very fastidious about her objects. She kept a lot of paper clutter, but every one of the knickknacks was always cleaned and dusted." Gwendolyn trailed her fingers over a red glass box etched with a stag at bay in a thicket. "I gave her that one for Christmas," she said, her voice dropping to a whisper. "I think she really liked it. You couldn't always tell with Mother …"

Gwendolyn walked into a slightly smaller room containing a neatly spread, full-size bed, Elinor's old mahogany dresser with its twin, coral-shaded lamps, and her collection of bottles and cosmetics on their mirror-surfaced tray. At the far end of the room was a closet flanked by bookshelves jammed with a hodgepodge of papers. The bedside table and the single chair next to the bureau were also heaped with letters and cards.

"That's Mother," Gwendolyn said, gesturing at the covered surfaces. "Just what I told you. She kept every note, every Christmas card that anyone ever sent her." She picked up a handful from the top of a bookshelf and riffled through them. "For some reason, she must have packed some of her old papers. Look," she said, turning to Thibodeau, "this is the birthday card I sent her just last month—her birthday was July 19—but here's a notice from the Atlanta Garden Club dated three years ago."

Thibodeau glanced at the stack. "I'd like you to sift through these, if you will, and see if there's anything from anyone you don't know or that looks unusual. Everything seemed pretty ordinary to me—looks as though she kept up with a few people back in Atlanta, and saved all the flyers and newsletters from her clubs and so forth. The books don't appear to have been pulled out."

"It all looks pretty normal to me."

Thibodeau picked up a packet of white envelopes secured with a rubber band that was lying in the bookcase on top of the books. He pulled a few out and looked in the opened edges. "She must have had at least one friend here in town. These were sent here in Boston to this address, starting just a couple of months ago. There's no return address or letters enclosed, just book reviews and literary articles. Ring a bell?" He handed them to Gwendolyn.

Gwendolyn took the packet. Each envelope was identical—an opaque, white, legal-size envelope addressed on a typewriter, the stamp placed precisely the same distance from the corners of each envelope.

"No, nothing," she said, passing them back after a brief

examination. "As far as I knew, she didn't have any friends in town. Maybe it's some literary group in the house … they have a lot of activities here, though I don't think Mother ever joined in, and they wouldn't mail things to each other. The way they're addressed is a little odd, don't you think? Using her full name … that seems pretty formal for people exchanging clippings."

Thibodeau looked through his typed report. "Everything's pretty much the way we found it. They did shut that window by the bed. It was open about twenty inches, it says here. They dusted for prints and photographed, then closed it."

Gwendolyn set the letters down on the dresser and went to the window. "That *is* odd. I know for a fact Mother never kept that window open. The fire escape is just outside, and she worried about it, even though I told her a hundred times that no one could jump up high enough to get hold of the ladder. And she wouldn't sleep in a draft. Someone else must have opened it."

"Says here that it was very hard to get down." Thibodeau pulled on the brass fittings. It took several tugs before he could raise the window up, and an equal effort to close it. "No way your mother would have been sliding that up and down very often. It's very possible the guy got out through here. If he knew your mother and knew her room, he could have taken the back elevator up from the basement without being seen, then gone out the window. I'll have someone question the neighbors in the back apartments. Keep looking, if you would, Miss MacGowan. Anything at all you notice could be useful."

The detectives stood back as Gwendolyn moved through the rooms and the bathroom. "No, nothing else," she said after she'd gone around twice. "Can I bring the papers back home with me? It would be easier to go through them there."

"No problem," said Thibodeau. The room will have to stay sealed for the time being, but I'll send someone over tomorrow morning to itemize what you take. Let's say ten. Come on, then, we'll give you a lift home."

Gwendolyn arrived promptly at ten the next morning and packed four cartons of Elinor's papers under the watchful eye of a young policewoman who counted each piece, making rapid notations in a stenographer's notebook.

Gwendolyn was ravenous by the time she got back home. She left the boxes in the living room and hurried to make herself a peanut butter and jelly sandwich and opened a can of fruit cocktail. She ate at the kitchen table and sighed, thinking about the mass of unwanted material awaiting her.

Closing the house after her father's death, Gwendolyn had been staggered by the welter of paper piled throughout the house and had been too dazed either to sort through it or throw it out. She had simply packed everything personal—loose papers, manila envelopes, small boxes—into larger moving boxes and shipped it all to her house, shipping Elinor's bits of furniture and special books to Copley Court.

Jefferson Davis and Elinor Buell MacGowan had led separate lives, and each had compulsively accumulated over forty year's documentation of those existences. Now a mountain of boxes crouched out there, bulging with society clips, letters from relatives, business associates, childhood photographs of Gwendolyn, of her parents, of *their* parents; phalanxes of aunts, uncles, cousins ad infinitum. In Gwendolyn's haste to quit Atlanta, she had packed the papers promiscuously, Jefferson's and Elinor's together, and she shuddered to think what might now be simmering in that unhappy stew.

After lunch she had gone rapidly through the boxes in the living room, relieved that most of what she found could be discarded. Elinor's flyers, announcements, ads, and unredeemed coupons made up the bulk of these papers. She set aside the first-class mail for later examination, but something about those banded envelopes kept nagging at her. Some vague memory was trying to surface, but Gwendolyn couldn't quite grasp it. Had she seen more of them in Atlanta? Were they packed somewhere in one of those boxes? To satisfy her curiosity, she decided to tackle the garage now. She brought out a container of trash bags and a box knife, threw both garage doors open wide, and reached for the first carton.

Now, Gwendolyn's knees ached, and her head was pounding. Standing and kneeling throughout the hot afternoon and into the warm August evening, she had filled plastic bag upon plastic bag with old check registers, flyers and coupons, and Xeroxes of her father's letters and memos. Jefferson—she shuddered at the memory—had been an inveterate writer of opinions to the local newspapers and commenter on books to his friends. At some point in the sixties, he discovered the copy machine and had taken to it like an alcoholic to a bottle, buying a state-of-the-art machine for his office and spewing out multiple Xeroxes of everything he wrote, mailing copies to an extended circle of recipients, who, to judge by their frequently perfunctory or uncomprehending replies were either bored or puzzled, and then would file all related correspondence, with batches of *extra* copies, in manila envelopes. Gwendolyn, her father's daughter, still kept a single copy of each letter and its replies.

Determining to stop after this box, she reached in and pulled out a worn Lord & Taylor gift box, about the right size for a sweater or shirt. It was jammed full of notes and scraps, most printed in pen in a thin, neat, sloping writing with no name following the salutation and no signature at the closing. In a second hand that she recognized as her mother's, each sheet had been dated at the top in pencil.

Mixed among them were ads and clippings with notations in the same neat, sloping writing. A music program, with Elinor's date, "12/29/50," had had the selections "Sweethearts," "Your Eyes Have Told Me So," "Don't Ask Me Why," and "I'll Always Be in Love With You" circled in the sender's pen.

The sender had also used a miscellany of stationery from hotels, railroads, and businesses, no two pieces alike. One note on Burlington Northern Railroad paper began, "Dear Heart: another of my foibles is riding railroad trains when possible, and still another is to steal a sheet of stationery for special purposes. And still another, on this sheet, at any rate, is writing to the girl I love. (There are many things you must learn about me.)" It gave Gwendolyn a queer turn to see an envelope had been postmarked years later—November 6, 1957.

Gwendolyn was puzzled. What in the world had her mother been doing? It didn't look like just a casual joke—not that many letters over years. Her fingers trailed over the sheets, and she picked out another letter dated 4/16/51. Picking a paragraph at random she read, "Make no mistake about it, Her care must be the best. He knows. There are so many things she wants. And he can certainly understand that. He will see that she will have what she needs. Again, he says: He understands, and he can care for her. And her NEEDS for care and relaxation are so extremely great right now."

It rambled on for several more pages, ending, "ys bb SA'd G C h w l t s w y thght a w u w y

i t m

   a   a

  l l

    a   t

    l   a"

The slanted strings of letters trailed on down to the end of the page. Gwendolyn calculated that this—whatever it was—was all going on two weeks before her own ninth birthday. She shuffled through more sheets, noting that many were written in the same kind of nonsense code. It was all just too bizarre, and she decided to take the box inside with her.

Now that darkness had fallen, the single overhead bulb made the garage seem isolated and exposed. She set out the filled trash bags, then checked the side entrance, snapped off the light, and locked the garage doors. As she walked across the dark lawn to the house, she glanced across the way at a car someone had left with its parking lights on.

Carroll Goslin sat hunched in his battered green Volvo and watched Gwendolyn's figure moving toward the house. Moments later, he saw a light flash on in the front bay window. For over an hour had sat immobile in the darkness, intent on Gwendolyn's movements. He was too far away to make out her features, observing only that she was tall, dark-haired, and wore mannish clothes. He gripped and released the steering wheel rhythmically, feeling the anger mounting within him. He had never forgotten the little girl in pigtails he had last seen in Atlanta thirty-seven years ago. It was because of her that Elinor had betrayed him … Elinor, who had promised to be his and who had broken that promise. He had finally dealt with Elinor, paid her back in some measure for those lost years, but revenge had brought him scant satisfaction. Even at the end she had never understood the enormity of her betrayal. The old woman smiling coquettishly at him Friday had been a schoolgirl anticipating a treat, not a woman fearing the hand of judgment.

He had been a fool to dream that there would ever be a life with Elinor, a fool to respond to her renewed approaches, to send her pieces of his heart once again, year after year. Hope renewed, he'd once more believed in their life together, refusing to consider her repeated treacheries. Her inability to love.

He pounded his thigh with a great, pale fist. "Fool!" a familiar, harsh voice grated in his head. "I knew you could never have her. *You* knew she had to die. You knew you'd never be free until she was dead." But Elinor *was* dead, and he was not free, he was *here*, huddled in a car, in the dark, staring at a stranger's house.

CHAPTER SIX

T he letters arrived on Wednesday.

Gwendolyn opened the larger of the two, a thick, white, legal-size envelope to find a sheaf of obituaries from all the Boston papers as well as the *Atlanta Journal*. There was no accompanying letter, no notation on the clippings, and no return address on the envelope, which bore a Boston postmark.

In nearly sixteen column inches, the *Journal* detailed Elinor MacGowan's shocking murder, incorporating a lengthy description of her social activities in Atlanta over the decades. Gwendolyn couldn't help but smile, knowing that her mother would have been thrilled to see she'd merited a lengthier obit than Jefferson.

Gwendolyn turned the envelope over in her hands, the Boston postmark reminding her of the packet of letters she had brought home from her mother's room. Again she felt a nagging tug at her memory. Now she had a vague image of having tossed similar packets into a box down in Atlanta. They had caught her attention at the time only because of their uniformity and because her mother had secured them with rubber bands. The majority of Elinor's correspondence was scattered helter-skelter about her bedroom and study in the old house with no discernible grouping or order.

Of course, Gwendolyn thought as she walked inside to the living room, it wasn't unusual for friends to send clips of obituaries to the family, but a friend always enclosed a little note or word of sympathy ... She set the envelope aside and slit open the second letter, on formal, gray stationery. The boldly inked black words on the pale, gray stationery were both startling and puzzling.

"We were deeply saddened to hear of the death of your father"—*My father?*—"and of the recent, tragic demise of your dear mother. I had heard that Jefferson passed away in 1985, but I was unable to contact you or your mother at the time, though I did try to locate you. I learned only that she had moved to Boston, but I had no way of reaching her since your telephone number, I was told, is unlisted.

"Perhaps you will remember that the last time I saw you, you were a young girl going through the 'horse crazy' phase. Do you remember that we went riding together once? I have always enjoyed that memory of our outing in Chastain Park.

"You may not know that I returned to England shortly after your father's retirement. I received a wire this past Saturday evening that told me of your mother's death and gave your address and phone number. The wire wasn't signed, but I assume that it was from you, and I want to thank you both for your kindness and delicacy of feeling in alerting me so quickly.

"We took the first available flight Monday and are staying here in Boston at the Park Regency. I hope you will call me at your earliest convenience. We are in room 1248. I must see you on a most urgent matter.

"Please accept Eric's and my deepest sympathy for your grievous loss.

Your friend,

Monica Colewell"

"… and I thought you ought to know about them, so I called you right away."

"Yes, it's an odd coincidence," Thibodeau agreed. "Bring them on down, and I'll have a look."

As she drove, Gwendolyn drifted back to that day in Chastain Park—nearly thirty years ago, now. She hadn't been back to the park since that afternoon, but it had been such an unusually happy day that it came back to her now, keenly and whole.

She could smell the newly mown grass on the open green. The sun was hot on her skin, but tongues of cooling breeze licked across her face and arms in delicious contrast as she moved. She was fourteen.

Her horse was fresh and a pleasure to handle. She had set him to a canter down a long, grassy slope and for the first time had gotten the knack of sitting to the pace. It was a sensual—and, she realized with a burst of amazement, a sexual—feeling, a smooth, driving, powerful surge that built to a near-climax right there in the park.

It was the last time she had seen Monica.

"She was one of my father's 'special' assistants," Gwendolyn explained over a cup of coffee at the McDonald's near the station house. "He always had a couple of secretaries or assistants on hand. There were lots of women interested in fabrics and textiles and the importing business, so he had plenty to choose from."

"What about this Monica?" asked Thibodeau.

"I really liked her. She was a tall gal, more striking than the pretty ones he usually preferred. I thought she was mature and sophisticated, but looking back, she couldn't have been much older than twenty-five or six. Of course, that's ages older when you're fourteen. She talked about all the riding she had done in England, and I loved her British accent. A lot of my father's favorites played up to me, but I thought Monica really liked me for myself. We went to a few movies together, and horseback riding—and once we almost went to a play together with my father. Lord, what a row that caused." Gwendolyn shook her head, pursing her lips.

"What happened?" Thibodeau asked, reflecting on the bizarreness of each new family situation.

"Oh, Mother threw a deep-dying conniption fit at the idea of the three of us being seen at a theater together without her. She was right, I suppose, but then she hadn't wanted to see the play herself. She had some other function she was going to, and there was the extra ticket. It was hell at the dinner table that night, and nobody got to see the play. Mother went out to her event, though."

"Was your father having an affair with this woman?"

"Probably, although I didn't think of things in those terms then. And that scene over Monica was just one of an endless series of rows over Dad's women, real and imagined. I think he had decided, long before I came along, that since Mother saw every casual conversation as an affair, it didn't matter what he did.

"Now I think some of his goings-on were attempts to have

some companionship. Of course, to be realistic, I'm sure there were real affairs, too. I can see now that most of the ones he singled out thought they were in line to be the next Mrs. Jefferson Davis MacGowan. It must have been a rude awakening for them to discover that, for whatever reason, he was indissolubly wedded to my mother. Always puzzled me, too, for that matter."

Gwendolyn stared into her mug. "Like the letter says, Monica left shortly after Dad retired—went back to England—but I know they kept in touch. Mother would be enraged each time she 'found' one of those airmail envelopes in his pocket, and on his side, he'd keep leaving them in his pockets to *be* found. He even made a few trips to England, oh, years later, which infuriated Mother beyond words."

"Who is this Eric she mentions?"

Gwendolyn avoided his gaze. "I don't know. That's really the reason I called you," she said slowly. "When I was quite a bit older, back around the time of those trips, there were more letters and more rows. I gathered that Monica had asked for money, for some family problem.

"I dreaded those arguments. And my father seemed to be waiting for some kind of doom to fall. One evening we were at dinner when the doorbell rang. The maid came in with a telegram. My father went pale and jumped up, still clutching his napkin. He stood there and said, 'The tiger has sprung.' The way he said it made my stomach go cold. It turned out not to be anything important, but from that time on, I waited for the tiger too."

"Sounds like you're still waiting," said Thibodeau, looking closely at Gwendolyn. "What about the other letter?"

Gwendolyn handed it to him. "It seems weird to me that someone would send these without a note. I've already gotten a few cards from friends here, and one or two have sent along the clippings, but that's normal."

"Nothing to pin down by the envelope," said Thibodeau. "Buy them in any Woolworth's. The Boston clips aren't too unusual, but the Atlanta paper is. Someone had to be keeping pretty close tabs on your mother to get it here this quickly. Did you send an obit to the papers?"

"No," said Gwendolyn. "I do happen to have one, but I hadn't sent it off, and it wouldn't have gotten down there and into the papers this quickly."

"And just how do you happen to have an obituary for your mother?" Thibodeau asked, raising his eyebrows.

"I suppose it would be odd for any other family," said Gwendolyn. "You see, my mother was quite ill a few years ago— she had viral pneumonia—the only time I'd ever known her to be sick. My father said the doctors thought she was terminal, so he asked me to come down to Atlanta, and when I got there he asked me to write up something for the papers. And I did. It was really more of a biographical sketch."

Gwendolyn gazed over Thibodeau's shoulder out the window. "Do you know what he did then? He decided she should look it over, so we drove down to the hospital, and he took it right into her room and handed it to her."

"Cripes! What did your mother do?"

"She pulled the oxygen tubes out of her nose, put on her bifocals, and began to proofread it. She was calling for a pen when I had to get out of there … But the point is, I didn't send mine out, and I didn't call the Atlanta paper."

⁜   ⁜   ⁜

Gwendolyn felt better while she was talking to Thibodeau, but her good mood evaporated as soon as she was alone again. They had agreed that she would make an appointment to meet Monica as soon as possible to find out why Elinor's death had drawn her back to the States so quickly. Thibodeau agreed that the papers in Gwendolyn's garage might be important and offered to help her go through the boxes. They had both been surprised when he also asked her to have dinner with him after she had talked to Monica. The thought of his invitation cheered her now and made the interview with Monica almost bearable.

The phone was ringing as Gwendolyn walked in the front door. Gwendolyn ran into the living room and snatched up the receiver. "Hello?" she gasped. There was no answer at the other end. "Hello?" Her voice rose in irritation. She decided to outwait whoever was on the other end and stood by the desk, phone to her ear, her hand over the mouthpiece. After nearly a minute, however, she realized that she would not outlast the silent caller and replaced the phone gently in its cradle.

Chapter Seven

The woman paused just long enough to light another cigarette, then continued her restless pacing about the narrow hotel room. She was a large woman, strong rather than heavy, and taller than the average man. The dim light that filtered through the heavy brown curtains reflected now and then off the thick coil of hair twisted about her head as she padded through the gloom. She was proud of her mane, its richness and luster, and kept it long, her sole concession to an otherwise damped and repressed femininity. She wore no jewelry, affected no makeup. Her dress was simple and severe: a tailored, tan linen jacket over a burgundy silk blouse, a matching linen skirt cut calf-length, heavy stockings, and deep maroon walking shoes of the type called "sensible."

On closer examination, her hair was, in fact, streaked with gray, and in a good light the lines about her eyes and neck would have accurately pinned her age in the late fifties, but one would first have been struck by her innate handsomeness. Her carriage was erect, though in motion she tilted slightly forward, as though leaning into whatever fate's next buffet would bring. A woman of restless energy, she never sat when she could stand, never stood still when she could be in motion. Now, chafing under the necessity of waiting for Jefferson's daughter, she paced ceaselessly about the room, trying to curb her impatience.

The pallor of the slender youth curled in the floral-patterned depths of an armchair contrasted markedly with the woman's robust health. Oblivious to the woman's movements, his pale eyes wide and unfocused, he seemed to float, immobile, like a medical museum embryo gazing out eternally from its jar. His wan face was framed by faded tow hair, poor, lank stuff that was cut in a ragged pageboy bob. One might have put his age at twelve or thirteen, but in truth, Eric Colewell was just two months short of his nineteenth birthday. Thin, white wrists pushed out of his dark-blue blazer, etiolated stems seeking light; a man's heavy wristwatch had slipped past his left wrist onto his hand. Knobs of bony ankles showed below his too-short gray flannels, his feet anchored in heavy, oxblood brogans. The sole of his left shoe was a good three-quarters of an inch thicker than its mate.

Monica Colewell paused by the bedside table and opened her massive black purse. She pulled out several sheets of crumpled yellow telegraph paper and reread them with the same rapt attention that she had given to the first and subsequent readings. Whoever had sent it to her had not stinted on expense, but had simply written it out as a letter and wired it in full.

"Dear Friend," it began.

"You will not yet have heard of the untimely death of Elinor Buell MacGowan, widow of the late Jefferson Davis MacGowan of Atlanta, Georgia.

"As one who is familiar with your situation, I knew you would want to know, as soon as possible, that she died recently in Boston, Massachusetts.

"I am assuming that you have known neither her, nor her daughter's whereabouts, and I enclose these for your information."

(There followed both Elinor's and Gwendolyn's addresses and Gwendolyn's phone number).

"I do not doubt that you will find a use for this information, and I wish you all good luck in your endeavors. I am taking the liberty of making reservations for you and your son at Heathrow for flight BA215 this Monday and have booked rooms at the Park Plaza for the two of you for a week starting Monday the 22nd. I assume that you will know within that time whether or not you will choose to extend your stay.

"My very best to you and your dear son Eric. A well-wisher."

This extraordinary cable had reached the Colewell household late Saturday evening, and Monica began immediately to pack. She had not paused to question the sender's identity or to speculate on his motives. Hers was a pragmatic nature, and she viewed the free tickets as her last chance to track down the Elinor MacGowan (or at least her daughter) who to all intents and purposes, had disappeared without a trace after Jefferson's death. The daughter had obviously not sent the wire, but since she would never have the chance to read it, Monica had written a gracious note of thanks upon their arrival, calculating that her cordiality would force the girl—she must be a middle-aged woman by now—to be at least civil in return.

"Eric, for God's sake, stop that!"

The boy, who by imperceptible degrees had raised his right hand to his mouth and was methodically gnawing his already bloody cuticles, slowly lowered his hand again. He neither looked at her nor protested her complaint.

Monica glared at her son, who continued to sit impassively in the chair. She sighed. He had barely moved since they had come back from lunch, but then, she expected little more of him. The boy dwelt perpetually in his own semisentient world, stubbornly withholding his thoughts and emotions. Sickly but not unintelligent, Eric had read rather more widely and thought rather more deeply than Monica realized, but his keen comprehension of his own frailty and of his utter dependence on this woman had led him to layer the bright core of his being with a dull, impenetrable shell. He spent his days attached, mollusklike, to his chair or bed, reading, dreaming—and resenting.

They led a secluded life in their rented cottage in Wantleigh, a small town about sixty miles west of London. Eric had been tutored at home, his health and their financial situation precluding travel or outings. In spite of his insularity, this sudden uprooting from his home had left the boy curiously unmoved. He had, if anything, been even more inert, totally disinterested in the plane trip, the new country, or even the view outside their twelfth-story window. He was simply there, the pale shadow of a spent passion rendered tangible. All too tangible, he had consumed Monica Colewell's life.

She turned back to the bedside table and rummaged in her bag for another pack of cigarettes. At the bottom of the black leather handbag were several thick packets of worn air letters tied with string. These bore as a return address a private box number in Atlanta, and amidst the reams of florid prose and bad poetry were promises of love and support for the child-to-be that Jefferson had unquestioningly accepted as his own.

Jefferson had been the last of a large brood of ragged children born to a small-town shopkeeper and his wife in a dot of a town in north central Mississippi. In his late teens he had moved to Atlanta and had struggled to put himself through Georgia State, determined to escape his past and to pass on something more to his own sons. Jefferson's five brothers either died early and violently, or produced, at best, a single girl-child or two. He confessed to Monica one night that he himself had had mumps when he was twenty-five, and feared that he would be unable to have children at all. He was proved potent by the birth of Gwendolyn, but his hopes for a male heir had been baulked when Elinor refused to consider a second pregnancy. Jefferson never forgave her, telling Monica that he had moved into his own wing of the big house in retaliation. He was childishly proud, after one of his English trips, to learn that Monica was pregnant with his child. He had been convinced that the MacGowan name would die with him, and in his joy at a possible renaissance, he hinted to Monica that should the child be a boy, it would not be too late for them to start a life together.

It was with foreboding, then, that she wrote to Jefferson about the baby's crippled foot and shortened leg. His other deficiencies—the heart murmur, the asthma attacks, the allergies—became apparent only as the boy grew older, but the distant tone of Jefferson's first, guarded reply killed any dreams Monica had entertained about becoming the next Mrs. Jefferson Davis MacGowan.

The blue airmail letters dwindled to a trickle—a Christmas note, a birthday greeting—and then ceased. Monica was left with the sole care of the sickly and uncommunicative boy. She also harbored an abiding hatred for Elinor and the child Gwendolyn, who, having Jefferson, possessed everything that she held dear. She tortured herself with thoughts of what might have been, and waited. At last there had come a sign. The cable.

She continued to pace, her mind turning a single thought over and over: I gave him a son, and that son will have his promised birthright.

Gwendolyn entered the hotel lobby with considerable trepidation. When she was fourteen, she had thought Monica a pretty good sort. She had felt sympathy for her father, whose, "But all we did was play tennis," or, "All we did was have lunch," seemed plausible and innocent enough to Gwendolyn the child.

But the years of clandestine letters and her father's solitary trips abroad had led Gwendolyn the adult to see things more from her mother's point of view. It would be galling to have continual reminders of one's husband's infidelity, even though Elinor had actively sought them, and Jefferson had passively allowed them to be found. Now, Gwendolyn didn't know what to think. What had happened to make this woman feel she could walk back into her life now?

Gwendolyn took some comfort in the fact that she had talked with Thibodeau this morning, in part to let him know about the meeting, but mainly for reassurance. He advised her to keep calm, to listen carefully to whatever Monica had to say, and to look forward to having a pleasant dinner with him afterward where he had told her to meet him at the Hong Kong restaurant in Harvard Square.

At the last minute, Gwendolyn veered away from the elevators and called up on the house phone, realizing that she had no desire to meet Monica on her own turf, or to be sequestered behind closed doors with her and whoever Eric might be.

The phone rang several times, and Gwendolyn grew impatient. Finally there was a click, a pause, and a low, British-accented voice said, "Monica Colewell speaking."

So clearly did the voice evoke the woman that it took Gwendolyn a few moments to regain her composure. "Monica? This is Gwendolyn. It's such a hot afternoon, I thought you might like to join me downstairs for something cold." Hot, cold, she was babbling, Gwendolyn chided herself. "The Captain's Quarters is just off the left of the lobby. I'll meet you at the entrance." She hung up without giving her guest a chance to refuse.

"Gaah," Gwendolyn murmured aloud, shaking her head. She made her way to the doorway and stood uncomfortably, shifting from foot to foot. She gazed up at the bar's garish sign. A paint-flaked graybeard—the Captain?—in a yellow slicker hat grinned into a gale wind, his still-lit pipe clenched between his teeth. The peeling paint overhead, the scallop shells, shellacked lobsters, buoys, and other nautical accouterments attached to the doorframe made Gwendolyn grit her teeth.

"The hell with it," she muttered and walked on in. The place was nearly deserted anyway, she reassured herself, and she wouldn't have any trouble spotting Monica, remembering how the young woman had towered over her. Gwendolyn chose a table near the back with lighting that would put her own face in shadow once she commandeered the wall seat. Monica would then be forced to take the chair lighted by the small overhead spot, where she would be clearly visible to Gwendolyn.

It was just after four, the hour designated as "Happy" by

the establishment. The bartender was opening what looked to Gwendolyn like a stainless-steel sarcophagus to display trays of tiny, wrinkled sausages and shriveled chicken livers wrapped in bacon. Gwendolyn decided to have something on hand as a diversion—"Have some hors d'oeuvres, Monica?"—and heaped an assortment onto a small plate. The bits had clearly done hard time in an industrial steamer before being skewered with toothpicks and released to the halfway homes of their chafing dishes.

A waitress decked out in a white middy blouse and black sailor's tie brought a bowl of pretzels and took Gwendolyn's order for a Molson's golden ale. She had just taken the first deep swallow when Monica walked up to the doorway. She hesitated, gazing about her nervously, and lit a cigarette. Gwendolyn let her stand while her own heart slowed its pounding and then she stood up and walked a few steps toward the door. "Monica?" she called, rather too loudly, "I'm over here."

Monica caught sight of her and strode quickly in. "I thought you said you were going to wait outside," she said brusquely. "Never mind. Where are you sitting?"

Gwendolyn realized that she had blundered and tried to recover lost ground. "I thought I'd get us a table before the crowd gets here." The words sounded fatuous even as she uttered them. The "crowd," so far, consisted of a heavy-set blue-haired woman nursing a gin and tonic, and two men in gray suits self-consciously sporting name tags from some hotel function. They realized simultaneously that their first conversation in thirty-two years was not getting off to an auspicious start.

"Gwendolyn, let me look at you," said Monica, her hearty voice overlapping Gwendolyn's; "Monica, it's been such a long time!" They stopped short, and Gwendolyn took the moment to introduce a neutral topic. "What would you like to drink? Come sit down and order. Would you like some hors d'oeuvres?" she finished, working in her prepared line.

Finally settled with food and drink, they smiled at one another warily, each searching for a way to open the conversation. Gwendolyn, who hated confrontations of any kind, felt faint with the effort but took the initiative. "Monica, it's wonderful to see you, of course, but why are you here? How did you hear about Mother? You thanked me for a telegram, but I never sent you one. Do you have it here with you?"

"Oh, I *am* sorry," said Monica, sipping her vodka and lime, "but I didn't think to bring it. We were off in such a rush, you see. It was an unexpected chance to see you and to help out in this distressing time. What did happen to Elinor, by the way? Was she ill long?"

Gwendolyn looked at her blankly. "Ill? The woman wasn't ill, Monica, she was murdered. Didn't your telegram tell you that?" They stared at one another. Gwendolyn felt Monica was lying about not having the telegram, but she could see that the murder came as a genuine shock. "Just what is it you want?"

Monica's brain was racing, trying to put all the pieces together. When she had let herself think at all about the possible origin of the cable and the tickets, it had been in a cloak of single-minded self-righteousness. She assumed that some ally—a friend of Jefferson's?—knew of her situation and wanted to help her snatch some share of the happiness that was hers by right. But this … Murder was more than she had bargained for.

"Killed! When? Have they found out who did it?" She leaned forward across the small table so suddenly that her drink slopped over onto the urethaned wood.

Gwendolyn shrank back involuntarily, her chair striking the wall behind her. What could she have been thinking to suggest this place? The bar seemed suddenly more confining than the hotel room could ever have been.

She steadied herself and blurted out, "Last Friday. Mother was found murdered at the residence where she'd been living here in Boston. She was shot, and she'd been pretty badly—cut ... They don't know who did it or why. I didn't send you anything, so somebody who knew pretty quickly must have had a reason for getting hold of you. You must have some idea who that would be."

"No, I don't," said Monica, truthfully, but her hand shook as she reached for a cigarette.

"Can we go up to your room?" asked Gwendolyn as the silence between them promised to stretch out indefinitely. "I think we have a lot more to talk over, and this isn't the place." The bar was finally beginning to fill up; footsore tourists and thirsty conventioneers were straggling in, crowding into the surrounding tables. Gwendolyn signaled the waitress for their check. "I'll pay," she said, dropping a five and two singles on the damp plastic tray.

They walked to the bank of elevators in silence, each wrapped in her own thoughts. Both had feelings of foreboding that they preferred not to share. As the elevator slowly ascended, one thought began to weigh on Gwendolyn, and the mounting tension in the claustrophobic elevator forced her to start speaking.

"Monica, give me some credit. I'm not fourteen anymore. You didn't come three thousand miles just to hold my hand, and I have a good idea of how you felt about my mother. If you don't know who sent the telegram, then you must at least have some idea why someone would alert you that Mother died. We're not going to get anywhere until you tell me what's up."

As Monica took a deep breath, the elevator doors swished open and they stepped out into a long hallway carpeted in gigantic red, blue, and gold paisley swirls. "To think that somebody got paid to design this." Gwendolyn laughed, a little hysterically. She could feel that Monica was about to tell her something, and she was quite sure that it was something she didn't want to hear.

"Gwendolyn," began Monica haltingly, "I don't know what you know about Jefferson and myself, but we were close."

"Yes, yes." Gwendolyn waved her hand dismissively. "I know as much about that as I want to. I had to hear about it quite enough at the dinner table. He visited you in England, too. But Father's dead. What about now? Why exactly are you here, in this hotel, and what do you want from me? In your letter you said 'we.' Who else is with you? Did your husband come too?"

Monica paused outside the door of room 1248. "No, not my husband, Gwendolyn. I never married. My son Eric is with me. My son ..." She fumbled a key out of her change purse and jabbed it into the lock. "*Our* son, Gwendolyn, Jefferson's and mine." Gwendolyn stood rooted on the threshold as her worst fears materialized before her eyes.

"Eric is your half brother," Monica plunged on, her voice harsh in defense of her child. She opened the door and walked in. "Eric! Eric?" Her voice faded and caught in a gasp. Her black purse lay gutted on the floor, and Eric Colewell was gone.

Chapter Eight

"It was simply unbelievable," Gwendolyn repeated for the third or fourth time—Thibodeau had lost count. He had been astounded when the heretofore cool, collected Gwendolyn Macgowan had burst into the Hong Kong a half an hour ago and began pouring out a confused tale of a brother—a half brother— and now, a *missing* half brother.

Thibodeau had ordered by stabbing at the menu held by the hovering waiter, and now tore his attention away from Gwendolyn as the server returned to set out their order. Thibodeau uncovered the first dish, and as the aroma of spareribs reached her nostrils, Gwendolyn sputtered to a stop, staring at the platter as though she had never seen food before.

"Why didn't you stop me? I've been babbling like a fool! I *never* do that! I'm starved!"

"Sounds like you've had enough this afternoon to make anyone babble. Go ahead—dig in."

Thibodeau smiled as she piled her plate with steamed dumplings, spareribs, and chicken wings and began systematically devouring them, stripping the meat off the ribs and gnawing the soft ends of the chicken bones. The waiter returned with two more platters and set them discretely next to Gwendolyn.

"Now you see why we detectives prefer to lock our subjects in interrogation rooms, than interview them in restaurants," laughed Thibodeau. "We'd go broke."

"I'm so sorry." She looked up guiltily. "I'm awful! I haven't said two words to you—just ranting on about Monica. But I feel … I don't know … like getting out of the doctor's office or through with a final exam. I'm just so glad to be away from that woman that I don't care what the doctor's report or the final grade is, though I'll be finding out soon enough, I expect."

"Well, it must have been an awful jolt to discover you have a half brother at this late date."

"Yes …" said Gwendolyn, brushing hoisin sauce on a pancake and covering it with moo shoo pork and a sprig of scallion, "and no. In a way, it's almost a relief to hear it for a fact and get it over with. My father went through so many peculiar relationships that something was bound to have happened. I remember one day when I was about fifteen, I was shopping in Lord & Taylor and one of the sales people who knew my mother asked after her—and my brother. I told her that I didn't have a brother, but she kept insisting there was one. It really shook me, and I figured she knew some family secret that I didn't know. Of course, she couldn't have meant this Eric; he wouldn't even have been born yet. But it became like my father and the tiger. I waited for it every day."

"Have another pancake," urged Thibodeau. "Take all you want. I was just kidding about the expense. We're here to eat, and I'm starved, too." He rolled a pancake for himself. "So what did you think about those phantom half siblings?"

"Usually, I was scared. I wanted to be the only one. Other

times, I thought I'd like to have someone else to talk to, and once in a while I got really angry that they might be living a happy life while I took all the screaming and arguing."

"Sounds like the MacGowan plantation was a fine place to grow up," commented Thibodeau mildly.

"I must make my parents sound like monsters," said Gwendolyn, "and that wasn't the whole picture, by any means. When I was just a kid my father taught me how to fly fish and took me camping, and Mother … well, Mother was difficult by anyone's standards. 'Strung high' my father used to call her behind her back. But I remember when I was just a little thing, she would make up stories just for me. One was about the Pink Spider—*me*—who was born to two ordinary brown spiders and was always in danger or getting in trouble because of her bright color. And I used to sit by her for hours while she played the piano and sang to me. 'All the Pretty Little Horses' was my favorite …" Gwendolyn broke off abruptly and touched her napkin to her eyes. She took a deep breath, then carefully spread the napkin back over her lap. She looked at Thibodeau, her eyes bright with unshed tears. "I loved to hear her play that piece. I'm sorry, this is all just too …"

"That's OK. I understand. Say, I've got an idea—"

Thibodeau signaled the waiter. "Would you pack the rest of this to go and give us the check?" He squeezed Gwendolyn's shoulders lightly. "Come on. I live just a few blocks away, and the walk will do you good. You can take the rest home with you."

"There, feeling better?" Gwendolyn nodded, not trusting her voice. The evening air was warm and comforting as they walked along Harvard Street. "Come on up and have a cup of coffee and talk a bit before you head back," urged Thibodeau. "We're nearly there now."

By the time they were settled in Thibodeau's living room, Gwendolyn had resumed her usual composure. "I'm sorry." She took a sip of coffee. "I hadn't gotten that shaky since Mother died. Or Father either, for that matter. Actually, I feel a lot better now. Sorry I spoiled our dinner."

"Don't worry about it, Gwendolyn. You didn't spoil anything, and really, you're entitled. Sometimes it's a little thing like a song or a sound that will hit you hardest."

Gwendolyn took another sip and let out a deep sigh. Even on this warm, evening, she found the hot coffee comforting.

"This is a very attractive place you've got here …" she broke off in embarrassment. "I don't know what to call you."

"Call me Warren," he laughed. "'Detective' is so formal, now that we've eaten Chinese food together." He smiled at her, and Gwendolyn smiled back as she looked around the tidy room with approval.

"Come on, I'll give you a Cook's tour of the place," he said, with the intention of keeping her mind occupied.

Warren Thibodeau lived in a modest, third-floor apartment in a four-story brick building that had so far escaped being "condoized." His apartment door opened onto a long hallway, off the left of which were a living room that looked out onto Harvard Street, a small study, and, at the far end of the hall, his bedroom. Doors to the right led into the kitchen, a linen closet, and a bathroom.

"And this is my library," Thibodeau said with a deprecating gesture into the study. "Not much golden oak, but all the books

I can cram in." The walls were solid pine shelving filled with volumes of all descriptions—fiction, history, biography, a sizable collection of telltale tan and red legal volumes, and numerous thick medical references. A lounge chair with a folded granny afghan, a goose-necked floor lamp by the chair, and a door-top desk on two file cabinets, a phone, and a battered office chair on castors were all wedged into what had been intended as a guest bedroom.

Gwendolyn looked over at the books appreciatively and then nodded at the lounger. "Doesn't look like you plan on much company either," she said, smiling again. She walked closer to the shelves, examining their contents.

"You know," Gwendolyn began, "it's funny about that house of mine. I really do love it. I love the idea of all the history it's seen and all the fine craftsmanship that went into it—that golden oak, for instance. But I know I'm just a tenant, a guardian. I looked up the records and found it was finished in early 1866. That means they were working on it while the Civil War was still going on. There were nineteen owners before me—and odds are that some of them died in their beds right there. At that period, JP was considered pretty far out from Boston. Folks would summer there to get away from the city heat. There'll probably be a few dozen after me, if the city doesn't raze the place for a parking lot. Everyone tells me there's too much space for one person—those three big floors and a full basement—but I have nineteen ghost lodgers for company. Besides, I do most of my living in the room you saw, where I can be near my books. If I go broke and have to move into a hovel, I'll find a hovel big enough to hold the books, even if I end up sleeping on stacks of them."

Thibodeau nodded. "I know what you mean," he said. "When

I was married, Ruth and I lived in a nice house up in Lynn. After she died—that was eleven years ago—" he hurried to explain, sensing Gwendolyn's unvoiced question, "I sold nearly everything we had and moved here. I kept all our books, though. They're a …"

"Necessity?" suggested Gwendolyn.

"Yes, that … and a comfort." He walked over to a shelf and pulled out a copy of T. H. White's *Once and Future King.* The book opened at his touch to a well-thumbed page. He hesitated, as though deciding whether to speak, and then explained, "Merlyn is talking to the young Arthur here, Gwendolyn, and he tells the boy, 'The best thing for being sad is to learn something. That is the only thing which the mind can never exhaust, never alienate, never be tortured by, and never dream of regretting.'" Thibodeau held the book open, but he knew the words by heart. "I agree with Merlyn," he finished simply.

"Yes, I do too …" said Gwendolyn. "Although I wonder about some of the things I've been learning lately. Still, I think it is better to know. Can we sit in here and talk? I like this room."

"Of course," said Thibodeau. "I'll go get our cups."

"Where do things stand now … *Warren?*" Gwendolyn asked when they were settled, she in the lounger and Thibodeau at his desk.

"To be blunt, we still have nothing. The open window is important, but there were no prints, only smears, and there is no indication that anyone searched or disturbed anything in the room. Like we said Sunday, it's possible that the killer knew her and knew her room—which would make it even weirder that she was killed in the basement—we checked, and her hair appointments are on Tuesday. How did he even know she'd be there? He either came in unnoticed, or she let him in; he killed her *there* for whatever reason, then went up the back elevator and out her window. None of that makes a very reasonable scenario. He'd risk being spotted going out that way, but those trees out in the alley are pretty thick by the fire escape. We're still questioning residents whose apartments overlook the alley. Evidently, they don't spend much time staring out at the trash barrels."

"You know, Warren," said Gwendolyn slowly, "there's something awfully odd about Monica getting that telegram so quickly. She's lying about something, but I didn't get it out of her with all the confusion about Eric. I know she was lying when she said she thought I sent it, but then she seemed genuinely upset when I told her Mother had been murdered. So, whoever sent it took pains both to send it immediately and not to explain the circumstances. And Monica's got to have some motive other than introducing me to my long-lost half brother."

"Money, I'd guess. That figures in somewhere on most things."

"Well, of course, I thought of that first, but surely my mother didn't leave her anything, and it's too late to get at my father's will; that finished up in probate this spring."

"But your mother's will hasn't been filed yet, and if Georgia is like Massachusetts, anyone has ninety days to file a claim on a will."

"Shit. Sorry. I hadn't thought of that. But how would she have any claim on Mother?"

"I don't know," conceded Thibodeau. "You'd better get hold of that lawyer in Atlanta and get the facts. She may not have a leg to stand on, but she could cause you a lot of grief and tie up the estate. Maybe she's partners with whoever sent the telegram. Did you see it?"

"No," said Gwendolyn. "I think she was lying about that too. She said she'd forgotten to bring it, but when she discovered Eric had gone through her purse before he ran away—if that's what the kid did—she was pretty upset about the fact that he'd taken a bunch of papers."

"Where's Monica now?" Thibodeau had been curious all evening but had wanted to see whether Gwendolyn would bring up the subject without his asking. His curiosity finally overcame him.

"I expect she's at her hotel. She was distraught about the boy but didn't want to call anybody—the police—about him, hoping he'd come back on his own. Besides, no one does anything for twenty-four hours anyway, do they, about a missing person? She said he's nearly nineteen, so no one would think it was odd for him to set out on his own in a new town. I told her I was going out to dinner and that I would ring her later. I'm not optimistic enough to think she'll disappear without trying to get whatever she came for, and she has my phone number, so I'm hardly in danger of losing her."

"I want you to keep me posted about whatever it is she wants. Do you know what the boy looks like? I can put out a few unofficial feelers."

"I haven't the faintest notion," said Gwendolyn. "Monica was going on about him being fragile and needing medication and so on, but all I know right now is that his name is Eric Colewell."

Gwendolyn stood up and stretched. "I'd better be getting back," she said. "Thank you for the coffee and the dinner. You know, there is something else," she said, sitting down again. "The other day, after I got back from showing you the letters and clippings, the phone was ringing when I came in. I answered it, but he—or whoever it was—didn't speak. I hung on for the longest time, and I never heard a sound, not a breath. But he was there. I could sense it. I know everyone gets odd calls, but it was unsettling—one more anonymous thing along with the clippings and the telegram—if the telegram really was unsigned. It seems to me that whoever killed my mother knew her, or at least had some reason for picking her rather than any other elderly woman in the residence. Would he have known Monica too? It would have to be from pretty far back, unless she sent some British hit man over to do her advance work, and even I'm not that paranoid."

"I've been thinking about those clippings," said Thibodeau. "They covered her whole stay at Copley Court and went back some months before she came north. Do you think you might have more that go back further? At some earlier point there may have been a letter or note with them."

"It's certainly possible," said Gwendolyn. "I've been vaguely remembering that I packed some batches of envelopes like that down in Atlanta. If memory serves, they were the same thing; typed, addressed with Mother's full name, and filled with clippings about social and literary types of things. Sunday evening I was poking around out there, and I found some very strange stuff from the fifties—actual letters, only in code and nonsense words. They were handwritten, and on all different kinds of stationery. I don't know whether they're connected to these envelopes or not. If they are, then this is someone who's known Mother for decades."

"I think Ed and I should definitely have a look as soon as possible—tomorrow? I want you to call me then, anyway, after you've talked with Monica, and let me know about the boy. I assume that if he isn't back at the hotel by morning, she'll want official help. Make sure she lets the people at the hotel know where she is. Where's your car? I'll walk you to it."

It was nearly eleven when Gwendolyn pulled into her driveway and parked in front of the garage. She was tired, but not as tired as the man behind the wheel of the green Volvo that had been parked in the shadows across the street for the past two hours.

He was a patient man, but he did not have great reserves of strength. Today's events had taxed him heavily. He patted the papers beside him on the front seat—yellow telegraphs and a packet of airmail letters. Behind him, covered with a blanket and silent now for the past several hours, was the gagged and trussed form of Eric Colewell.

CHAPTER NINE

A terrible pain tore across Eric's lips, and he struggled to open his eyes. Air … not enough air … someone slapped his cheek. And then, again. He groaned, but his breathing steadied. He tried to focus on the huge, gray shape looming above him. "Wh … wh?"

A hand clapped over his mouth, and a voice hissed in his ear, "Don't scream—not in *her* room—or I'll tape your mouth again."

His head immobilized by the huge, damp hand covering his mouth and jaw, Eric could only glance about. Beyond the man he saw a pair of piercing blue eyes radiating naked hatred directly into him. Alarmed, he realized after a moment that he was looking at a painting on the opposite wall. The portrait created a third presence, as alive as either of them. Eric would have found her handsome if the artist had not allowed her soul to escape through the eyes. Mesmerized by the ferocity of her gaze, he relaxed in the man's grasp.

"I'm going to take my hand away. If you cry for help, you will regret it deeply. Do you understand?"

Eric nodded, tearing his gaze away from the painting, and when the man stepped back, he turned his head and looked about him. The painting was the single decoration in a vast room that otherwise contained simply a bed, a nightstand with a small lamp, a television set off to one side, and the chair in which he was sitting. The objects looked like toys some giant, careless child had strewn about in the cavernous room.

As his mind cleared, he decided the man's warning was unnecessary—he could hear no traffic or other outside noise, and the tall windows were heavily curtained. And the man was right there, waiting to grab him.

Eric ran his tongue around his chapped lips. He tasted the salty sweat from the man's palm, and his stomach lurched. "I'm thirsty," he whispered, then, suddenly aware of an urgent fullness, "and I have to go to the bathroom." He looked up at his captor.

The man grunted noncommittally and then pulled him to his feet, steadying him by the elbow. He escorted Eric to a door that opened directly off the bedroom and pushed him inside. "Get it over with." When Eric looked at him without moving, the man colored and turned his head. "Go on, I'm not looking at you."

Eric finished up and washed his hands, cupping them under the faucet to drink great draughts of water. When he came out, the man closed the bathroom door and locked it, putting the key in his pocket. Eric obediently sat back down as the man motioned to the chair.

"I will get you something to eat." He announced this formally, as though Eric were the young master and he the devoted servant. He locked the outside door as well.

Eric didn't move until the man returned. He bore a tray laid with a cloth mat and linen napkin, sterling silverware, and little silver salt and pepper shakers. Eric's stomach growled at the sight of the handled cup of creamed soup and matching white china plate with a quartered and crust-trimmed chicken salad sandwich resting on fresh lettuce leaves. Filling the entire length of the tray was the largest knife Eric had ever seen.

"Sit on the bed."

Eric did as he was told.

The man placed the tray on the bedside table, removing the knife. He turned the chair toward the bed and sat down, resting the flat of the blade across his thighs, running his thumb slowly back and forth across its thick spine. He nodded at Eric to begin.

Out of habit, Eric put the napkin on his lap before beginning to spoon soup into his mouth. The first taste roused him to a frenzy of hunger. He tipped up the cup and drained the thick liquid, then gobbled down the morsels of sandwich and the greens, his eyes traveling between the silent man and the cold, painted face on the wall. The man's eyes mirrored the woman's, but instead of her focused hatred they held an emptiness he'd only seen on the telly in old Val Lewton horror films.

He looked up apprehensively at the man then, cautiously drew his legs up and lay back on the bed, his head sinking into the large, yielding pillows. Eric remembered that he hadn't taken his medications but realized he also hadn't coughed or sneezed for hours. He had never felt so terrified in his life—or so alive.

"No, Eric never came back to the hotel. Monica is here with me at the house, and she wants to report him missing." Gwendolyn had rung up Thibodeau at eight in the morning, in part to help Monica, who was frantic with worry, but primarily to hear any voice other than Monica's. The woman was distraught, babbling nonstop, yet she talked about the boy as though he were a valuable piece of property that she didn't want damaged. That might well be the case, Gwendolyn reflected; without Eric, could she make any claim on the estate, if that, indeed, was her intention?

"I wondered, since you and Ed are coming over anyway, if she could make the report to you instead of going downtown? She has his passport photo here with her. Fortunately, she had both passports and her traveler's checks in her suitcase."

"Okay, I'll talk to her. I'll see you two about nine thirty."

Gwendolyn hung up and wondered what in the world to do with this large, weepy woman for the next hour and a half. The phone had been ringing when she came back from Thibodeau's last night. This time there was no silent listener, who by contrast would have been far preferable, but rather a highly vocal Monica, beside herself and begging for Gwendolyn's company. To spare herself a night in a strange hotel room with *this*, Gwendolyn had suggested Monica wait overnight in case Eric came back on his own. Then, if he still hadn't returned, she could cab out to the house. Monica had appeared on her doorstep, bag in hand, at six thirty-five.

Ironic, Gwendolyn could not help observing, that in less than twenty-four hours, Monica had managed to insinuate herself into her house—something her Mother hadn't accomplished in nearly two years. *Lucky for Monica, my guilt must have built up to critical mass, and she was the final atom*, Gwendolyn thought. *Someday I'll learn to say no and mean it.*

"Let's go out back and sit on the patio," Gwendolyn suggested in desperation. "I'll make us a pot of tea, and we can talk while we wait for the detectives." Monica let herself be led out onto the wide flagstone terrace directly off the kitchen. She plopped down on one of the rickety benches at the redwood picnic table.

"Not much of a table," said Gwendolyn apologetically. "I keep meaning to get one of those nice wrought-iron sets." With this, her store of small talk was exhausted, and she fled to the kitchen, taking as long as possible to prepare a pot of strong Lapsang Souchong. Rattled, it took her several trips to organize a full complement of cups, spoons, sugar, and milk.

"Do you have lemon?" asked Monica plaintively as Gwendolyn prepared to sit down. Overnight, Monica had mutated from garrulous to girlish, a change Gwendolyn felt ill became a woman nearly six feet tall.

Gwendolyn sighed and disappeared into the kitchen, returning shortly with a bottle of Realemon. "The closest I've got," she said, sitting down to her own tea. Monica pointedly poured milk into her cup. They sat for long minutes in silence. Gwendolyn flicked a black beetle off her saucer. "Tell me some more about Eric. After all, he's my half brother. Has he ever run away like this before?"

"Don't be silly. Of course not," Monica replied in a wounded tone. "He's been ill so often," she explained, as though illness and togetherness were somehow equated. "Besides, we enjoy one another's company and prefer to spend most of our time together. Oh, sometimes he goes to the cinema, but most often we spend the evenings watching telly or chatting."

"How about the days?" Gwendolyn found herself actually becoming interested. What would life full-time with Monica be like? "Do you have a job?"

"When Eric was born," Monica answered, warming to the subject, "my parents were still alive, and my mother took care of him while I went back to work at the firm where I met Jefferson. They made fabrics, as you know, woolens and tweeds and so forth, for export. Later on, I switched departments and learned to do advertising and layout work. Now I have a minicomputer, and I can work at home doing the same kinds of things."

"Doesn't Eric have any young friends?" Gwendolyn pictured the bleak days rolling on, the boy, then man, and his mother closeted together year after year …

"No. Eric is a shy lad, and I think he really prefers to stay at home most of the time. He reads a lot, and there is a library within walking distance that he often goes to."

Conversation lagged. Monica's eyes filled with tears, and Gwendolyn looked away hastily, unable to think of anything comforting to say. She was sick to death of civility, of Monica's problems, and of this still phantom but time-consuming half brother. Gwendolyn racked her brain for some reasonable excuse to leave and go inside. She sprang to her feet in relief when she heard a car pull into the driveway.

"Good morning," she called out eagerly as Thibodeau and Albano got out of the car. "Monica, these are detectives Warren Thibodeau and Ed Albano." Gwendolyn nodded to the two in turn. "Warren, Ed—Monica Colewell. Can I offer the two of you some coffee or tea?"

"I could stand a cup of coffee, but none for Ed, I'm afraid," said Thibodeau. "Mrs. Colewell is going to have to go downtown after all. We'll need to make copies of the photo of the boy to distribute, and we want her to look at some mug shots of known sex offenders. A desk clerk noticed Eric talking to a man in the lobby. There's no reason to think you'd ever have seen any of these guys," he said, turning to Monica, "but we need to check it out.

The clerk gave us a description. Not much to go on—tall, pale, late fifties, early sixties. We've had her go through them too, but she couldn't make any IDs."

Monica, pale and drawn, nodded mutely. She went into the house to get her purse and the passport and then got into the car with Albano.

"Now," said Thibodeau to Gwendolyn with a grin, "how about that coffee?"

When they were seated outside at the table, Thibodeau asked to see the packet of white envelopes that Gwendolyn had brought back from Elinor's room.

"They're the only thing out of the ordinary that we have to go on right now," he explained, "and they're too much like the envelope you got with the obituaries to be coincidental, I think."

"I agree. Mother opened them all, so I presume she read them or at least looked at what was inside, and the fact that she kept them all together instead of just piling them around means they had some importance in that disorganized world of hers." Gwendolyn pushed back from the table. "Instead of just talking, why don't we go tackle the stuff in the garage? We can see what else there is and go over it all together."

"I feel like a ten-pound brick is being lifted off my back every time I throw something away," commented Gwendolyn, brushing a damp strand of hair off her forehead. The heat hadn't broken, and by ten thirty the two were wringing wet. Thibodeau had taken off his jacket and rolled up his shirtsleeves, and his face and forearms were coated with grime.

By the time they broke for lunch, Gwendolyn was tired and discouraged. They had waded through boxes of scrapbooks detailing Elinor's triumphs, boxes of plaques, awards, and citations from service clubs and organizations extolling Jefferson's years of civic efforts, but found nothing revealing. She culled the loose photos from each box, and was now appalled at the jostling crowd of strangers staring up at her from the mounds of prints.

Some were funny, some poignant: a sepia snap of her parents holding hands by an old Model A on their honeymoon showed the two as a couple of skinny, grinning children half Gwendolyn's age. What off-roads and bypaths had they taken, she wondered, to become these strangers whose lives she was trying to decipher here in a garage, so many miles and years from that snapshot? Most of the subjects, however, like a twentyish young man in a straw hat sitting on a donkey, were anonymous faces in unknown locations smiling or frowning out of their frozen moment in time.

"Who were all those people!" exclaimed Gwendolyn in exasperation.

"What?"

"Oh, just wondering out loud. All these photographs. Could these people all be related to me? They must be. I can't imagine even my parents keeping this many random photos."

"Makes me feel like an orphan," remarked Thibodeau, catching up a handful and flipping through them.

"What do you mean?"

"I think my folks have about three photos of me and my brother, and outside of their wedding picture on the mantel, I don't think there's any other record of either of their families. The Thibodeaus must have stepped off the boat with just their toothbrushes and left their Kodaks back in Toulon."

Gwendolyn laughed. "You know, you have a way of making me feel much better. It's a lot easier with you here; at least it's an even match, not two to one. Does the police department really think there might be something in all this stuff to warrant sending one of their finest out for the day?"

"Frankly, I don't know. But the way your mother was killed makes me believe she had some previous connection with the killer. I can see a junkie with a gun, and I can see a nutcase with a knife, but when someone takes the time to use them both, that's more like revenge to me. That means someone who knew her earlier, and this is the only place to find a connection."

"I understand what you're saying," said Gwendolyn, "but if it was someone she knew, and assuming she hadn't just pushed one of her housemates beyond his limits why didn't he kill her down in Atlanta? Why follow her up here?"

"Yeah. It kind of falls down there," conceded Thibodeau. "Still, we don't have anything else but the open window, and no one we've questioned in the area saw anyone on the fire escape. Even if he did leave that way, and that seems plausible to me, he didn't leave any prints, so we know only that he figured a clever way out, not what his motive was or who he is."

"It tells us that he knew where her room was," said Gwendolyn thoughtfully. "I doubt he asked her first and then killed her."

"Wait a minute," said Thibodeau. He got up and retrieved his jacket from the garage and then sat back down and pulled the packet of white envelopes from his inside pocket where he had placed them earlier.

"What is it?" asked Gwendolyn. She pushed the plates and glasses aside and moved around next to him.

Thibodeau was spreading out the envelopes and arranging them by date. "Look," he said, tapping two of them with his forefinger. "I'd been concentrating too hard on what was inside them. When I first flipped through them I noticed that they were postmarked 'Boston,' but look at the first ones. They were mailed from Boston to Atlanta and then forwarded by the post office to her new address. The latest ones are from earlier this year—a couple of months ago—from Boston to her Copley Court address."

Gwendolyn leaned closer to look at one of the dates. "March, 1985. That's before Mother moved up here. It went to a post office box in Atlanta. Before my father died. This one from January of this year went to Atlanta and back here. He—if it's a he—must have been sending her mail in Atlanta and didn't know that she'd moved."

"He did by June," Thibodeau pointed out, holding out another envelope. "It's postmarked 'Boston' and addressed to her at Copley Court. I wonder if she ever answered it? Did your mother have an address book?"

"Yes, she did. A thick, black one she'd had for ages. But I didn't see it in her room, and I didn't even think to look for it. I'm sure I didn't pack it with her papers—it was something she'd have kept with her."

"The killer could have taken it on his way out. If it had been there, our men would have found it. But I'll have someone go back and double-check right away. May I use your phone?"

"Sure," said Gwendolyn. "There's one on the wall just inside the kitchen door. And the bathroom's just outside the kitchen on the right, if you want to wash up."

"That feels a lot better," said a damp Thibodeau emerging from the house a quarter of an hour later. "They'll go over her rooms with a fine-tooth comb looking for the address book. You know it amazes me how much your mother did. I got the impression that your folks just fought or philandered."

"That's my fault. My dad was an excellent businessman, but Mother really had a lot of different talents. She published her own book, and she really did love learning and books. That little collection of Faulkner first editions in her room is just the tip of the iceberg. I had to rent a storage locker for the others. Brains, or book-learnin' brains at least, weren't particularly prized among her Southern social set. But she could do that, too, when she wanted to. She could turn on the charm like nobody's business, and they went to all the symphony and opera balls. She was very highly thought of by a lot of people."

"Doesn't follow that no one liked her at the home …"

"You've hit it on the nose. The 'home.' Nice as it was, she thought of Copley Court as an old folks' home inhabited by a lot of nobodies. If you couldn't further her aims, she didn't want to know you. She was sugar and spice to the head of a board of directors, but she could cut you off at the knees without your feeling it till you tried to walk, if she didn't need you anymore."

"Sounds monstrous!"

"It seems that way, but think a minute: Women didn't have it so great up north either, but Southern women, once they'd been set on their pedestals, were totally ignored. I'm convinced Dad fell in love with her because she was bright and smart and witty, but then he couldn't bear it when she had the same traits as a wife."

Gwendolyn paused, shaking her head. "Probably why I never wanted to get married. Gave me the shudders …"

"And now?"

Gwendolyn scrambled to her feet. "Let's get back to the garage. I have a feeling we're going to hit pay dirt. You go on ahead—I want to get something I left upstairs." When Gwendolyn returned with the Lord & Taylor box, Thibodeau was already digging through another parcel of photographs.

"Come look at these. They're the weird letters I was telling you about. The dates start back in the early fifties, then stop after a few years, and here's one from 1980. Maybe there's something even later. I never got to finish looking at them. Ha!" Gwendolyn held up a plain white envelope with a handwritten address. "Mother's dated this one November 23, 1981. And there are just clippings in it, no name, no note."

"There's some sort of progression," agreed Thibodeau. "If your mother kept all of these letters, and if she was as thorough as she seems to have been about dating them, then somewhere in this mess we ought to find the link."

Gwendolyn returned the letters to the gift box and dragged another carton out into the yard in the sunlight. As soon as she opened it, she felt waves of unpleasant energy. Reluctantly she picked up the first white envelope and pulled out the yellowed onionskin paper. The precise, printed words struck her like a physical blow:

"I made you what you have become today, yet through your vanity and sickness you have chosen to deny your friends and to seek fame and glory on your own.

"But there is no fame, no glory, only worms, only hollowness, only your lies.

"I will tell them of your falseness, I will strip you of your pride, I will …"

Gwendolyn set down the fragile paper, her hand shaking. The very sun seemed gray and unclean, and her stomach lurched as though she were going to vomit. "Warren," she called hoarsely. "Warren!"

CHAPTER TEN

E ric huddled naked under the cool sheets in the center of the big double bed. It might be Friday morning—or afternoon—he had no way of knowing. He peered over the side of the bed and saw his shoes, a sock tucked neatly into each one. He had no memory of falling asleep or of being undressed and put to bed. He had been awake for some time now, listening in vain for any indication of life, but there was no stirring of household activity, no sound of traffic or passersby in the street. He was alone with the portrait and its scalding gaze.

Where were his clothes? There was a door that might have opened into a closet next to the bathroom, but he didn't dare get out of the bed. The man had locked the bathroom door, and even if the bedroom door had been open, he wouldn't have dreamed of venturing out into this house alone. He noticed a drawer in the bedside table and pulled it open. Inside were a worn, leather-bound King James Bible and a book. He took out the book, eager for any diversion. The dust jacket was done in gaudy shades of mauve and red, a sunset casting an entwined couple into silhouette. It was a novel, *The Ceremony of Innocence*, by Evelyn Dulac.

One page had been torn out, but on the title page was an inscription in faded ink, "Til it is Temple Time Forever, I C W T S W Y, A M L, Evie."

As Eric idly flipped the pages, a snapshot slipped out into his lap. Its edges were deckled, as though it had been cut out with pinking shears. A pretty woman with waved hair was standing next to a much taller, long-faced man. He had dark hair and in the monochrome photograph his complexion was almost white. He stood stiffly by the woman, clasping his hat in front of him with both hands. He looked unusual, rather than handsome. Eric looked closer and realized that the man in the photo was the man with the knife. For a moment the paper eyes held his, and in their own way were as pitiless as those of the woman on the wall. He looked away and thrust the photograph back into the book. He placed the volume back just as he thought he'd found it in the drawer, terrified that the man might slip in and catch him with it.

Carroll Goslin sat at his oak desk, rocking back and forth as he hummed, tight-lipped, fighting to clear his mind. He had been at the Park Regency yesterday afternoon watching for Gwendolyn, as he had each day since Monica's arrival. Instead of his comfortable black coat he had worn a tan sport jacket with patches on the elbows. Goslin had found that his prominent, pale features passed for "scholarly pallor" if he wore normal clothes, and, as he expected, no one in the lobby had given him a second glance as he waited in ambush behind a morning *Herald*.

He was finally rewarded Thursday afternoon by a glimpse of Gwendolyn and Monica's awkward meeting, and for an instant he toyed with the idea of following the pair into the Captain's Corner. Discretion prevailed, but he willed the interview to go badly for them both. Years ago Goslin had hated Monica's smug assumption of Jefferson's affections, while he himself yearned unrequitedly after Elinor. He had never forgiven Monica for calling him "Caroline" behind his back—nor Elinor for repeating the remark to him in her tinkling laugh, as though he would find it amusing as well. He had kept track of Monica's whereabouts and had wired Monica on Friday, counting that envy and greed would lure her to Boston bearing some cargo of misery to Gwendolyn's doorstep and, in the long run, disappointment, humiliation—or worse—to herself.

Gloating turned to dismay when he saw the frail boy limping by, carrying a sheaf of papers. When Goslin heard the boy's British accent as he asked for a candy bar at the newsstand and recognized the yellow sheets of the cablegram, he knew it had to be Eric. Instinctively he called out to him, and when the boy came up to him, Goslin trumped up a story about Monica and hustled him out a side entrance and into his car.

Goslin didn't understand why the boy was carrying the cable, but he couldn't risk any connection being made between the cable and him. He had met Monica at one and another of the MacGowan galas, and there was the remote possibility that she would recognize him now. Jefferson might well have told Monica all about him, as he had had to hear about Monica ad nauseum during Elinor's tirades. Elinor had informed him of Eric's birth, and he, too, had been spitefully pleased that the bastard son was defective. Now the boy was here in his own home—in Mother's room—he thought with a spasm of guilt. And really, it was all Gwendolyn's fault …

Mother had told him when he first met Elinor that she would bring him pain. At the time, he'd thought her jealous and spiteful, but she had been proved right. Mother. She had warned him even before Elinor; had forbidden him to go study in New York, vividly painting dangers awaiting him there. He had ignored her, hearing only her rage and desperation at his abandonment.

"Is it worth my unhappiness to leave me for a whole summer?" she shrilled endlessly, sarcastic and abusive, wounding him deeply, as always, with surgical precision. "It's a waste of time, Carly. You'll never be a writer, never amount to a hill of beans. Keep your library job. Stay home with me—where you belong."

"I'll just be taking two courses at the university—and I've always wanted to see New York. They've read my stories and must think they're worth something—they accepted me. You know how much this means to me," he begged, revolted by his cringing, whining self.

"They'd accept anyone who sent them the application fee," she'd snapped and turned away, sending him to Coventry for the rest of that day.

The more he defended himself, the more she railed on and on, unable—unwilling—to veil the malice in her ice-blue eyes at the thought of him living alone in New York, out from under her thumb for two long months.

Another time: "You'll be out running around every night!"

"Like I am here?" Carroll replied bitterly. She drew in her breath at this outright rebellion. She glared but held her tongue. That was one argument she couldn't use against him, he'd thought, ruefully. He was never out of her sight long enough to "run around." She clutched him to her while thrusting him away, like a cat embracing its prey with its front paws while disemboweling it with its hind claws. Mother despised him, scarcely endured his company, but fed on his weaknesses and needed to keep him bound to her.

Until that summer, Carroll had viewed himself solely through his mother's eyes as an incompetent weakling. It was only after being accepted for the summer short-story writing seminar at Columbia that he looked in the mirror and for the first time saw a tall, slender young man, not a rugged outdoorsman by any means, but someone who might well pass for an academic in the university classes. Someone who might actually achieve his dream.

And so that summer marked his first separation from Boston and Mother. He had yearned for it enough to withstand the weeks of tears, reproaches, and guilt, and as he boarded the train at South Station he knew that New York would bring him a wonderful new life.

It brought him Elinor.

New York was sweltering in late June, but it was glorious to twenty-three-year-old Carroll Goslin. He roamed the university campus in the soft dawns, and in the steamy evenings rode the subway downtown to prowl through Greenwich Village. Between classes he ate his sandwich lunches in Riverside Park, always listening, watching, jotting down his observations and snatches of overheard conversations in the notebook he carried with him everywhere. He rejoiced over every filled page, convinced he was finally launched on his life as a Writer.

There were only nine people in his short-story class, and from the first Carroll was attracted to an outgoing older woman whom he guessed to be in her late thirties. He watched her, covertly at first, and then, despite his extreme shyness, spoke to her one day after class.

"I liked the piece you read," he stammered, "the way you handled color and sound ..."

"Why, thank you." She had a pleasing Southern accent and responded to his attention. "I'd never heard anything of mine read aloud, before," she confided.

She then suggested they go out for coffee, and from that moment on they spent every spare moment together. They were bursting with book talk and writing talk, and each felt empathy for another whose family "didn't understand" the need to write, the love of books. They pored over their lecture notes together, encouraged each other's ideas, and laughed at the other students' lesser efforts. They ate cheap food in cheap restaurants, lingering late over cheap red wine. They gloried in it all. They became lovers.

But by degrees, Carroll became aware that it was Elinor's work—not his—that was consistently singled out by the professor. It was Elinor who finished up her stories early while he labored endless hours trying to find the perfect order for the perfect words. It came so easily to her, he thought ruefully. She had a flair for dialogue that he would never master. Her prose was flamboyant, but she somehow made it work, like the ridiculous hats she wore with such panache. Carroll felt a pang each time he heard her work praised.

"Look, Carroll!" Elinor exclaimed one day, waving a sheaf of papers. "It's the first chapter of my novel!"

Novel? Carroll was taken aback. So far, he had thought no further than his short stories, had never aspired to anything as ambitious as a book, and here Elinor had typed out an entire chapter in addition to her assigned class work. Elinor's enthusiasm was infectious, however, and Carroll was quickly won over to her project. He offered suggestions for settings and characters, most of which Elinor took gratefully, incorporating them into her expanding manuscript. Dialogue continued to be her forte, and she let it carry her story, often falling short on plot and detail that the more methodical Carroll was happy to supply.

As their affair grew more intense, Carroll, as a joke, began mailing little notes to her apartment, written in a kind of shorthand. Elinor was tickled by his attentions and responded in kind. Their code evolved, like Egyptian hieroglyphics down through the dynasties, until they could communicate many things with single letters. "I L Y" would obviously be, "I love you," but longer strings like "I C W T S W Y T," were quickly understood to mean "I can't wait to sleep with you tonight."

As they said their good-byes at the end of the course, Elinor invited Carroll to come to Atlanta over the Christmas holidays. She laughed at his feeble protests, waving them away with her familiar airy gesture. "Nonsense. Jefferson will be delighted that I'll have someone to escort me to all those lovely holiday events that he so detests."

Elinor, as usual, proved right. Far from being suspicious of the young man, Jefferson gave Carroll a tour of the city, showed him through his importing operations, and was indeed delighted to be spared the conjugal rites of eggnog galas, symphony balls, and opera dinners. Carroll, in turn, was grateful for the MacGowans' hospitality and dazzled by the vast spectrum of social events to which Elinor introduced him. His head was kept in too great a spin to allow his shyness to surface, and he thoroughly enjoyed himself, gaining in just two weeks a veneer of polish and sophistication. He did not dwell on Mother, alone in Boston—her rage at losing her Carly over Christmas for the first time in his life had produced arguments of titanic proportions—and he accepted that there would be similar consequences upon his return.

"Who are you?" Eric ventured. He was eating a small veal chop that the man had cut into bite-sized portions for him. The man had entered the room abruptly (Eric shuddered at the thought of having been caught examining the book and photo), allowed him to use the bathroom, and then brought in a tray of food with a spoon as the sole utensil.

"I know your mother."

"Where is she?"

The man didn't bother to answer. He sat in the same chair. He held the same sharp knife on his lap, its patterned surface rippling like watered silk as he turned the blade over and over. Fascinated, Eric wondered if the man thought he would leap out of bed and overpower him if he entered unarmed. That outlandish image almost made him smile.

The man held up the packet of airmail letters and the telegram. "What were you doing with these?" he demanded, keeping his voice neutral. "Where were you going yesterday?"

Eric choked on his mouthful of milk, and stinging tears came to his eyes. The cold fear that had been a small ball in his stomach spread cancerously through his body, chilling his limbs.

"Nothing ... nowhere ..." he managed to whisper. "I was angry at my mother. She wouldn't tell me what was going on or why we were here. So I went through her pocketbook." His voice grew stronger as his resentment returned. "She's always going over those bloody letters, and I thought I'd get even by taking them while she was gone and reading them myself. I just wanted to get away from her for a while. I wanted to get out of that room ..." His voice trailed off.

"And did you read them?"

"No," Eric replied, averting his gaze. "I had just come downstairs when you called to me. What are they, anyway? Why are they so important—is that why you brought me here?"

"They are from your father. He tells your mother that he will marry her, and then, after he learns of your birth, he tells her, oh not in so many words, but he tells her that he will not marry her. He was a liar and a betrayer, like his wife."

Eric flushed and angrily pulled himself up in the bed, forgetting that he was naked. Flustered, he yanked the covers up to his armpits. "My mother is not a liar!"

"I didn't say your mother was a liar. I said your father's wife was a liar and betrayer."

"My father was an American. He was killed in the Vietnam War," Eric recited as though by rote. Tears welled up in his eyes. "They were married. Mother told me so."

"Mothers are often less than truthful," the man replied. "But that is of no importance now. I must go out tonight, and since I cannot leave you here alone, you will come with me. You will be tied and gagged, and if you resist me in any way, I promise I will kill you."

Gwendolyn poured herself a chilled Bally ale and sat back in the window seat in a futile attempt to relax. The coroner had called just as she had found the threatening letter to tell her that Elinor's body could be released. Gwendolyn had left at once to make arrangements, promising Thibodeau that she would call him later in the evening.

It was Friday, one week to the day since Elinor had been murdered. Gwendolyn had called the funeral home to arrange for the body to be picked up and then went downtown. The coroner's assistant had handed her a small paper bag with Elinor's effects: the gold watch with two small diamonds—a gift from Jefferson— the gold-link bracelet and heavy fretwork silver ring set with a purple stone that her mother had worn during her last moments alive. As she signed the release for cremation, Gwendolyn had realized with finality that her mother was truly gone.

Elinor was to be cremated and buried in Atlanta beside her husband. No stone had yet been erected for Jefferson, Gwendolyn reflected. She rolled the cold liquid slowly over her tongue, wondering what possible inscription she could devise for a tombstone embracing them both.

Gwendolyn put down her drink. It was making her restless, rather than soothing her, so she got up and wandered into the kitchen and on out into the backyard. Monica was asleep upstairs in one of the front bedrooms, having been delivered to the house shortly after Gwendolyn had returned from the morgue. According to the patrolman who accompanied her to the door, Monica had become so distraught at the station that they had had taken her to the ER at Mass General and had her seen by a physician who prescribed a mild sedative. She had taken two tablets and was already drowsy when she came in the door. Gwendolyn helped her into bed, hoping she would stay quiet for the rest of the evening.

Now, as she walked restlessly in the twilight, Gwendolyn felt a need for company, even Monica's. She felt a rush of sympathy for the woman, who must feel as alone and bereft as she, and decided to go up and see whether she was awake. *Perhaps she'd like a bit of dinner,* Gwendolyn thought, feeling more kindly toward her. Monica hadn't eaten much this morning, it was unlikely she'd had a good lunch, and it was getting late. Dusk was falling. She opened the bedroom door and called softly, "Monica?"

"Mmmm …" said a sleepy voice. "Come in. I woke up a while ago … I was just dozing. I'm a little groggy."

"I thought you might be hungry," said Gwendolyn. "I'm going to fix something for myself—would you like to come down in a while and join me?"

"Why, thank you," said Monica. "Yes. I'll just wash up and put on something fresh."

Gwendolyn felt more cheerful once they were both seated outside in the warm evening air. She had made up her mind to be as gracious as she could to her guest, and had prepared an attractive spread unlike her usual catch-as-catch-can cuisine: crabmeat salad on lettuce leaves, a dish of olives and mixed pickles, deviled eggs, hard rolls, and sweet iced tea.

"Tell me about Eric." Gwendolyn passed Monica a plate.

"Maybe it will help to talk about it. I know this must be hard on you. Have they learned anything more?"

Monica put down her fork. Her eyes misted, but she made an effort at control. "No," she said in a low voice. "Just what they said this morning when the detectives were here. A woman at the newsstand saw him talking to a man, but all she could remember was that the man was tall and pale."

"What were they doing?" Gwendolyn asked.

"The girl couldn't remember," said Monica, taking a tentative bite of crabmeat. "She only noticed Eric because he had come over to the counter to get a candy bar. Another customer came up directly after Eric, so she doesn't remember much else. She thinks the man called out to Eric, but she couldn't actually remember what name he called. What am I going to do? He's all I've got, Gwen."

Gwendolyn hated to be called "Gwen," but she bit her tongue and went on, as soothingly as she could manage, "Don't you think it's time to tell me why you came? If you'll be honest with me, maybe we can work together to find Eric. Who sent the telegram? Who has a reason to bring you here to Boston and what was in it for you to make you come without writing me first, if it really was me whom you wanted to see?"

Monica looked her in the eye. "Money. Money, and recognition for Eric and myself." She hesitated. "Revenge, really, to tell the truth. I've hated you all these years, you and your mother. You kept me from what I wanted most, you know, the happiness I could have had with Jefferson. If we had married, Eric would have had a father, and I would have had a life. Do you know what it's been like, year after year with that boy? Withdrawn, ailing? I think he hates me, and I'd almost grown to hate him too. Or I thought so until yesterday.

"I've never been separated from Eric. He is my child. I chose to have him, even if I did think then that it was my only way to keep Jefferson. But Eric didn't ask to be born, and he hasn't had any better a time of it than I have. What will I do without him?"

"We don't know that you've lost him yet, Monica." Gwendolyn could feel the muscles in her temples tighten, but she kept her voice steady. "Listen to me. Do you think you were the only woman who believed my father was going to leave everything for her? Do you know how often I was used by his girlfriends—or whatever it was that he called them? And Monica, I don't think it had all that much to do with me—or Mother—anyway. He loved having a wife, a child, and a position. If he had left—or divorced her—for you or anyone else, he would have had to give all that up, and I don't think he could have faced the loss."

"But he kept in touch for so long. He came to England, he wrote me letters. He wanted a son." Monica seemed unable to comprehend Gwendolyn's words.

"But not any son, evidently," said Gwendolyn, straining to keep her voice neutral. "Monica, I'm not trying to hurt you, but if Father had really wanted a son that badly, he would have left us and gone to you. But what would he have done in England? And how could he have brought you and Eric—even if he had been born perfect—back to Atlanta? He would have jeopardized the image it had taken him a lifetime to build. Don't you think all this has gone through my mind a thousand times too? Oh, not about you and Eric," Gwendolyn went on as Monica started to speak, "but about why my parents stayed together at all. I can only think that however much was wrong, their marriage gave them more of what they needed than a separation would have."

Monica stood up and began to pace about the patio. "What do you mean, 'what they *needed*'?"

"It's hard to put into words." Gwendolyn spoke slowly, as though explaining the situation to herself. "I guess I mean that there were a lot of things that could have made them happy, but that they opted for what would give them status or at least kept the status quo. It was too risky to give up their respective positions and strike out into something new and frightening. My father adored going out alone fly-fishing for example, but he just gave it up. Who knows? He might have been gloriously happy with you and Eric in a little English village with heaths and trout streams—if there are any left in England. But that's not your fault or mine, Monica."

They sat silently, listening to the night sounds. There was a kelpy tang in the air wafting off the harbor. In the distance, thunder rumbled faintly. "Feels like it's going to rain tonight," said Gwendolyn to change the subject. "We'll talk some more later, Monica. Just relax while I run inside for a minute. I told Warren—Detective Thibodeau—I'd give him a call, and I don't want to let it get too late. Don't bother about the dishes," she added as Monica made motions toward helping. "I'll bring them in later."

Goslin parked his car in the shadows enveloping Beech Hill. He figured it was no more than a hundred and fifty feet, through the trees and beyond, onto the patio by the side of the house. He cut the lights and left the driver's door unlocked. Eric lay tied in the backseat, covered with a blanket.

Goslin's forehead was beaded with sweat, his mind racing but clear. He hadn't brought the gun tonight; there was no guarantee that he would get a clear shot, and he was no marksman. Until the moment came last week, he hadn't even known he would actually use the gun. But the knife … the knife felt quick and alive in his hand—and it was silent.

He slipped through the maze of black tree trunks until he was crouched behind the boxwood hedge that bordered the drive. A gibbous moon was rising, silvering the roof of the garage and house, and splashing the flagstones on the patio, but the heavy foliage obscured the ground beneath the beeches, and it was just a short dash across to the patio.

She was sitting at the table, her back to him. The moon streaked highlights onto her dark hair, while the light from the kitchen cast her in silhouette. The only discernible movement was the rise and fall of the glowing end of her cigarette.

Goslin wore an old pair of tennis shoes he had found in the back of his closet, a dark pair of loose trousers, and a black sweater. He backtracked through the trees and crossed the driveway down near the front of the house, creeping along the grass border. The sound of thunder was rolling closer, and the air tasted of salt, heavy with the coming rain. He paused at the corner of the house, some fifteen feet behind the woman.

He turned the knife over in his hand, edge uppermost, a thin, lethal line in the moonlight. He forced himself to take deep, steady breaths to clear his mind. He rocked on the balls of his feet to steady himself and then rushed forward, rapidly covering the distance.

Goslin wrapped his large hand around the woman's face, covering her eyes and nose, yanking her head back and dragging the blade across her throat before she had time to cry out. Hot, black blood gushed over his wrist and hand, splashing onto the table. With a tremendous burst of force, the woman threw herself up and back, so tall she nearly toppled him over, and upsetting the bench. She gave a whistling gasp as she fell. Goslin, trembling, regained his balance, the knife slippery in his shaking grasp, a stain spreading down his pants leg. Unmindful now of the noise he made, he crashed headlong through the box hedge running through the trees toward the car. Just as he cleared their trunks and reached the sidewalk, a woman's voice called from the house.

"Monica! Would you like some tea?"

CHAPTER ELEVEN

E ric heard the thud of running feet. The man wrenched the car door open, and in the few seconds it took him to struggle into the driver's seat and turn the key in the ignition, Eric heard someone call his mother's name, then a scream that was silenced by the slam of the car door. Eric felt raw waves of terror and excitement flowing from his captor.

The promised rain burst, drops pattering on the windshield lightly, then pelting in blinding sheets, loud against the roof. The already humid air became suffocating, and, under the heavy blanket, Eric was drenched with sweat. Cold fear stabbed his stomach as the car swayed and skidded on the slick pavement. Over the hammering of the rain, the man moaned continuously from the depths of a despair more terrifying than his rage.

Despite the heat, Eric's teeth began to chatter. His body shook with fear as he was thrown back and forth on the seat. There was a squeal of brakes and the receding sound of a horn. The car bumped up over the curb, and the man wrenched it back, throwing Eric onto the floor of the backseat. His head bounced against the floor, and he bit his tongue, a spurt of metallic blood choking him as he fought against the gag.

At last the car slowed, turned sharply, and came to a halt. Gasping in great, dry, racking sobs, the man hurled himself from the car. Eric heard the car door slam, then, moments later, the door to a building.

As time passed, Eric stopped trembling and forced himself to think. Clearly, something terrible had happened. He was sure he had heard a woman call his mother's name moments before the man had returned to the car—then he had heard that scream.

During the journey, Eric's face had scraped back and forth on the car floor enough to loosen one corner of the tape over his mouth. Now he lifted his head and began to rub his jaw against the welted edge of the seat. It took several minutes, but he was able to peel off the tape. He spat out blood onto the floor and ran his bitten tongue over his dry lips.

He didn't dare yell for fear of attracting the man's attention, so he decided instead to get himself back up onto the seat. He was lying on his right side—the stronger—and was able to get enough purchase to raise his chest a few inches. A wave of nausea engulfed him, and he fell back panting. He fought panic, knowing with certainty that if he didn't get himself out of the car, the man would return and kill him.

With a second effort, Eric hitched himself up enough to be able to rest his elbows on top of the seat. He could feel some slack in the cord about his wrists, and bore down on his elbows to maneuver his feet under him as best he could. He pushed up with all the strength remaining in his right leg, and slid his buttocks up onto the seat. Once upright, he rubbed his forehead against the front seat and dragged off the blindfold.

He seemed to be in a kind of alley behind rows of brick buildings. Through the rain he could see other parked cars and rows of garbage cans on the left of the car; a Dumpster blocked his view to the right. The cord on his wrists was looser, but he still was unable to free his hands.

He felt the choking panic rising again, but he willed himself to be calm. Time was passing. The man could come for him any moment. He had to get out of the car. He was grateful that the man hadn't tied his feet—perhaps he'd figured it didn't matter with a cripple. That thought produced a surge of anger. Eric slid over to the right side of the seat and grasped the door handle behind him in his bound hands. The door opened part way and banged against the Dumpster. Eric half-slid, half-fell onto his back on the wet pavement. He rolled over, and by putting his forehead on the ground and inching his knees forward, managed to raise himself to a kneeling, then upright, position.

He stood panting for a minute, then nudged the door closed with his chest in case the man should look out to check the car. He walked behind the big metal container. It was difficult to see, with the rain pelting down, but there was a light over one of the back entrances that dimly illuminated the back of the Dumpster. There were two protruding rods above his reach, but then he noticed a jagged tab ripped out near the bottom of the container. Eric crouched down with his back to the sharp tongue of metal and tentatively rubbed the cord against it, producing a slight give. He sawed more vigorously, cutting flesh as well as cord, and the twine gave way. Eric struggled to his feet, rubbing his bleeding wrists.

He peered out from behind the Dumpster, and, seeing no one nearby, hastened out of the alley with a gait as near a run as he had ever managed.

Eric wandered blindly through the rain without having any concept of time. He was soaked and shivering, his slacks and thin, short-sleeved shirt plastered to his body. At some point the rain cleared his head, and he stopped at an intersection looking about in confusion. He realized he had been crying. Traffic was rushing along to his left in a steady stream, and he walked in the same direction. To his right was a double street divided by a wide esplanade, while across the stream of traffic was some sort of a fenced park. He wiped the hair out of his eyes and trudged on.

The doorman at the Ritz Carlton Hotel eyed him contemptuously. Eric gazed yearningly past him into the brightly lit lobby but didn't dare try to enter in his bedraggled condition. Passersby snug under their umbrellas gave him a wide berth as they hastened by. He wished he could remember the name or the location of his own hotel, but he knew he would look ridiculous asking the whereabouts of an unknown hotel from one of these well-dressed people. Eric came to another busy intersection. There was only one sign visible, indicating that at least one of the two was Arlington Street, and he trudged on, looking for some suitable refuge. At the next block Eric glanced to his right and saw a lighted Greyhound bus station, and he rushed indoors seeking the safety of a crowd.

He thought he would find the men's room and dry off, but when he pushed open the door, two men looked up from something they were doing in so menacing a fashion that Eric quickly backed out and hastened upstairs. He went into a Burger King at the front of the station and got into line. He listened to the man ahead of him order and said quickly, "I'll have the same thing, please—and is there a telephone nearby?" he rushed on before the girl could turn away, "and how much does it cost to use? I'm new here," he added, unnecessarily.

"Just a dime, kid. Ten cents."

Eric pulled out the bills he had taken from Monica's wallet. "Could you give me change?"

"Your order's two thirty-seven," she said, pushing the tray at him. When Eric just stood there, she took three singles out of his hand and counted out his change. "Here. Three cents, a dime—the little silver one—and two quarters. Phone's outside the door."

Eric took his tray to a table in the back corner, where he could watch the entrance. He sat down and realized that despite his fear, he was ravenous. He attacked the burger and chips. It was thin and greasy and delicious, and the potatoes heavily salted. He gulped down the cold drink and took a deep breath. He felt much better. It had been cold outside in the rain, but indoors, the rain had turned the atmosphere hot and steamy. He stopped shivering.

Eric stood up and fished a sodden piece of paper out of his pocket. He smoothed it out on the table in front of him. He was thankful now that he had taken some money out of his mother's pocketbook and that he had copied down the names that he had found on the cable. Experience had taught him to write down any potentially useful information he ran across. Eric took the paper and the dime and went out to the phone booth. He dropped in the dime and dialed the number, his heart hammering. A woman's voice answered. It sounded as though she were upset or had been crying.

"Mrs. MacGowan?" he read off the paper. "My name is Eric Colewell."

"I keep wanting to wash my hands," said Gwendolyn, rubbing her palms across her knees. "When I went outside the rain was just starting to come down. These big, heavy drops were splashing on the table, and there was blood all over everything, on the table and on the plates, in the food … So much blood I could smell it. And when the rain hit the blood it made it splash. Blood was splashing up off the table … and then I saw Monica … How can I tell the boy?" She drew her knees up to her chest and wrapped her arms around them.

Thibodeau and a uniformed officer sat across from Gwendolyn in the straight chairs as Gwendolyn huddled on the couch.

"I only went in for a few moments to call you," she continued, looking uncomprehendingly at Thibodeau, and … and … I just don't know." She put her forehead on her knees and began to cry.

Gravel crunched as a car pulled into the driveway. "That'll be the boy," said Thibodeau. "Are you up to this?"

Gwendolyn looked up and nodded, wiping her forearm across her eyes. They walked to the front door and met Eric as he was escorted in by the patrolman.

"Eric … I'm Gwendolyn MacGowan. Come on in."

The boy looked young and small and frightened. Could he really be nineteen? Involuntarily, she reached out and took his hand, looking at his stick-thin arm and wrist, and drew him into the hallway. "Why, you're soaking wet," she said, taking in his clinging shirt and muddy-kneed slacks.

"We're going to have to get his statement," said Thibodeau. "Bring him into the living room."

"First we're going to get him into some dry clothes," Gwendolyn insisted. "We won't be a moment. Come on, Eric." The adrenaline that had enabled Eric to escape from the car had drained away, clouding his ability to think or resist. He let himself be led upstairs.

"Something happened to my mother, didn't it," he said softly as they walked into the bedroom. It was a statement of fact, not a question. Monica's overnight bag still lay open on the dresser, and the clothes she had taken off before dinner were strewn on the bed.

"Eric, I …" Gwendolyn broke off, at a loss for words.

"I was in his car … He stopped and got out. I heard someone call Mother's name … then a scream. Please tell me what happened, Mrs. MacGowan."

"I'm not Mrs. MacGowan. Just call me Gwendolyn. And get out of those wet things—there's a bathroom over there. You can put on some of my pajamas. I'll find you some proper clothes in the morning." She looked at the boy and faltered. "I'm not trying to avoid your question, Eric, but it's better if you talk to the officers downstairs first."

Even with the elastic waistband, the pajama bottoms drooped around Eric's narrow hips. Gwendolyn rolled up the cuffs on the legs and sleeves and gave the boy a pair of thick socks to wear as slippers.

"Let's go downstairs. Detective Thibodeau will explain everything, and he needs to hear your story.

Eric veered back towards the bathroom.

"I think I'm going to throw up …"

CHAPTER TWELVE

After Eric had rid his system of the last vestiges of burger and fries, Gwendolyn washed his face with a cold washcloth. For the first time, she noticed that his wrists were still bleeding where he had been bound. She had him wash them thoroughly in warm, soapy water. She patted his hands dry, then peered into the medicine cabinet. "I don't think I have any Band-Aids ... Ah. Here–"

Gwendolyn opened a tube of Bacitracin and holding Eric's left hand squirted out a dab onto his wrist. As she rubbed the ointment over the abrasions, tears rolled down the boy's cheeks.

"Does that hurt?" Gwendolyn paused, concerned.

Eric shook his head. "My watch. It was my father's. I lost it ... I ... I couldn't go back ..."

"Maybe they'll find it ..." Her words sounded empty even as she uttered them. Dear God––if only it *were* just a matter of a lost watch ... She spread the antibiotic on his other wrist then gave him a quick pat on the shoulder.

"All right. Let's go downstairs. Tell your story while it's fresh in your mind. I'll fix this room up for ..." Gwendolyn hesitated a fraction of a second ... "You'll be staying here with me, now."

Eric made no response to this statement, but allowed himself to be led downstairs and settled on the living room couch. Gwendolyn went out to the patio, where Thibodeau was conferring with the forensic team, and motioned him in.

"I'll be upstairs," she announced to no one in particular. Eric remained unresponsive, huddled on the couch while Thibodeau stood gazing down at him. Several long moments passed before the boy looked up. Then, fixing Thibodeau with his pale, blue gaze, he demanded: "Tell me what happened to my mother."

"I wish there were anything else I could tell you, son. She's dead. She –"

"He killed her, didn't he," Eric said flatly.

"Yes. She was murdered—here—this afternoon …

Eric clamped his hands over his eyes. He shuddered and hunched over, arms pulled tight against his chest, his body racked with sobs.

"I'm so sorry …" Thibodeau began to sweat. He rubbed the back of his hand across his brow. "I'm just so damned *sorry*— believe me. But I need your help, Eric. I need it *now*. It can't wait till tomorrow. I need you to tell me exactly what happened while you were with that man. Anything you can remember might help us catch your mother's killer."

Eric continued to cry in great, heaving gulps, rocking back and forth.

Thibodeau sat down on the couch and reached out to the boy, but as his fingers touched Eric's shoulder, the boy jerked away. Then, after a final, shuddering sob, Eric lowered his hands and sat up straight. He swiped his tears away with a clownish swath of Gwendolyn's drooping pajama sleeve and faced Thibodeau.

"Please. I want to help."

"He's asleep. Finally," said Gwendolyn, coming into the living room. Thibodeau was slouched on the couch, his legs stretched out, ankles crossed, staring straight ahead at—nothing.

"You need to go home. Get some sleep," she added when Thibodeau didn't respond.

Thibodeau shook himself back into the present and patted the cushion next to him. Gwendolyn sank down with a sigh. It was after two in the morning, and except for a uniformed officer detailed to watch the house for the night, the rest of the entourage, the panoply of violent death, had dispersed.

"Thank you for being here," Gwendolyn said.

"How're you holding up?"

How should she answer that?

After finding Monica's bloody corpse, she'd stumbled into the house and dialed 911. Then Thibodeau, just to hear his voice. To her great relief, he had come at once. And now had stayed on until she'd settled Eric. She had tucked the boy into bed then sat by him, listening, murmuring comforting noises as he alternately cried for this mother, then raged against her for treating him as a child, then became wracked with guilt. "I could have done something … if I'd known why we came …" She'd massaged his hands and wrists with fresh ointment until the boy began to breathe evenly and deeply, whispering … "them to find my watch …" as he fell asleep.

How *was* she holding up?

"OK, I guess," she managed. I must be more tired than I realized—I seem to have promised Eric he'll be staying here with me."

"Wish you hadn't?"

"Not exactly ... but, I just *blurted* it out."

"We'll find out if he has any close relatives, and see what they want to do. He's an adult, after all ... though I doubt he could fend for himself. He looked about seven in those pajamas. That reminds me—their suitcases have ben released. I'll drop them by tomorrow."

"Did he give you any useful information?"

Thibodeau reached for his notepad, flipping through it as he talked.

"Said the guy is very tall—though you've got to remember that Eric isn't even as tall as you are—very pale, and has large hands. Again, the kid's so thin that my hands would wrap around his arm, too. Here—I'll read it to you. From the hotel:

–I heard someone call my name.

–You mean he called you "Eric?"

–Yes. He said "Eric," and I went over to him without thinking. We were in a hotel lobby ... it never occurred to me ...

–Then?

–He said that he was an old friend of my father's—my father was an American, you see—and that he was going to take us, my mother and me, to his house for dinner. He said Mother had gone ahead with his wife to get some groceries and that we were going to join them. I believed him, so I followed him out to his car and got in.

–Didn't that seem odd to you?

–No. Maybe it should have, but Mother never explained anything she did. She never even told me why we were coming to the States. That's why I took the cable and letters.

–Tell me about those.

–Mother got a cable last Saturday evening, and then she started packing and said we were going to Boston. When we got here I was angry that she hadn't told me anything—I can think, you know. I could be some help if she'd let me ... Could have been ...

–And so?

–Then she went downstairs to meet somebody. She took her wallet but left her purse. I went through the purse and took some money and the letters and the cable.

–What were you planning to do? Did you read them?

–No, I didn't have time. I was afraid Mother might come back and catch me, so before I went down, I copied out the names and phone number in the cable and skimmed it—it was about some woman dying here, and about the tickets and hotel. I didn't look at the letters. I don't know what I was going to do, exactly. I thought I'd go outside where I could be alone and read everything. But then the man called me.

–Can you describe him for me?

–He was very tall, and he had very big hands. When he grabbed me later his hand went all the way around my arm, and another time his hand felt like it covered most of my head when he put it over my mouth. They were very white, and the veins were very blue. His head was large too, and he had big, dark eyes and a high forehead. His hair was a dark brown, but going gray. It's hard to say, because in one way he was odd-looking, and in another, very ordinary. He had on a jacket and tie, nothing I remember very well. I think the jacket was brown and the tie dark brown or maroon.

Thibodeau looked up from his notes. "That ring any bells?"

"No," replied Gwendolyn shaking her head. "Nothing. Keep reading."

–What happened when you got outside?

–He said he lived somewhere with "North" in it. "North Shore," I think. He asked me if I liked the ocean. When I said yes, he said that his house was on the ocean. We drove through a lot of traffic, and then out on a point of land overlooking the ocean. We parked, and he told me to get out to look at the waves. Then he grabbed me. There was no one around … it happened so quickly. He was much stronger than I, and before I knew it, I was tied and in the backseat. He put something over my mouth and eyes. There was a long time when we drove around, and then I was in that room. I must have fainted—I couldn't breathe properly.

–Can you describe the room?

–It was large, bigger than any in our house, tall windows all covered with dark drapes. The man said not to yell. The ceiling was real high. There was a big painting on the wall facing the bed. A really terrible-looking woman. I mean, the woman looked all right, but her eyes were scary. There was a chair—the man sat there to watch me eat. He always had a large knife, and he just sat there watching me and kept rubbing his hand up and down the blade. There was the bed I slept in, and a table by the bed. I found a Bible and a book in the drawer in the table. There was a photograph of a man and a woman in the book, and I think the book was called something about innocence …

"Warren!" Gwendolyn interrupted. "That must be Mother's book. It was called *The Ceremony of Innocence*. If he had that, he *must* have known her …"

"Do you have a copy?"

Gwendolyn looked away. "No. It's embarrassing, but I don't keep one in the house. The whole subject of her writing caused such tension at home that I didn't keep my copy—she signed one to me. I looked through it then put it back with her books. I don't know if she noticed … It was a period romance, sort of a pre-Harlequin. Lots of heaving bosom. But it sold. It had a flashy cover, I remember. I packed hers—and mine—in one of the boxes out in the garage. Maybe the manuscript of that second book is out there too."

"I think all the answers are out in those boxes. We just have to keep at it."

Gwendolyn jumped up from the couch, running a hand through her already disheveled hair. "For God's sake, Warren, what's going on? Why now? Who would want to kill Monica? How did they even know she was here?"

"I think it's a *he*, not a *they*, and it's the same guy that grabbed Eric. He probably mistook Monica for you. I'd go so far as to bet he sent that telegram to Monica as well—it's too much coincidence, otherwise—but why, I can't even guess."

"If he's the one who sent it, then he must be from Atlanta— that's the only way he'd know both of them. But *who*? And why would he be here in Boston?"

"It would be just barely feasible," mused Thibodeau, "although admittedly crazy, for someone—our killer—to have lured Monica over here with the idea of getting at some of your mother's money. But even in that scenario, no one would have killed the goose before getting the golden egg. Someone must have been watching one or both of you two, though, to have come here to the house."

"It all gives me the creeps. I think I'll have a drink. Want one? I have some beer and a bottle of Jack Daniel's. I need *something*."

"You go ahead, Gwen. My brain says yes, but my ulcer says no. I shouldn't even drink this much coffee."

Gwendolyn fetched the bottle and a cut-glass tumbler, savoring

Thibodeau's "Gwen," and for the first time in her life rather liked the sound of it. She took a healthy swig of whiskey. "Will you and Albano be working on this case too?"

"Most likely. Jamaica Plain isn't in our jurisdiction, but Elinor's and Monica's deaths are obviously related, so we'll probably be loaned out for this one, too."

Gwendolyn walked over to the bay window and looked out onto the moon-dappled lawn. "It looks so peaceful out there," she said, feeling the bourbon start to work. "Would you read me the guy's description again?

Thibodeau obligingly paged back and read the lines again.

"Damn. Nothing. I can't think of any business acquaintance or any of my clients …" Gwendolyn emptied her glass.

"Poor kid was upset when I asked about a license plate later on in our talk—got mad at himself that he didn't think to get it, then cried about that damned watch he lost, then back on about the plate. Took me quite a while to convince him it was better to have gotten away alive."

"Poor kid is right," said Gwendolyn. "And what's worse is that watch is probably something Monica trumped up. My father left them flat, and I don't see him sending any watch."

"In a way, I hope we don't find it, then. Not likely since Eric was so turned around that he has no idea where he ended up. It has to be somewhere nearby, though, for him to have walked to the Greyhound station. He sure didn't walk back from Revere. A lot of big old homes and a lot of alleys in this area, though, but pretty well-combed. Anything shiny or valuable would have been snatched up quick."

Gwendolyn yawned. Thibodeau smiled for the first time that evening.

"Go get some sleep. We can start in again in the garage tomorrow morning—let's say eleven. Sleep—and a good breakfast; I'll be here in my old crawling-on-the-floor clothes." They walked down the hall, and as he opened the door, Thibodeau reached over and squeezed Gwendolyn's hand. "I'll see you tomorrow … *today* …"

It was three o'clock in the morning, but Carroll Goslin was not asleep. He had roamed through the darkened house, up and down the staircase, until he was exhausted. Now he sat in the chair in Mother's room, lulled by the sound of his even breathing—until he felt the portrait's eyes upon him. Mother.

She was right—he never had amounted to a hill of beans. He still lived in her house, held in trust in her maiden name years after her death, still lived off her money. He had never written a book, never held a job other than the menial position at the library. Thanks to her, he had never wanted for money, but he had also never known the independence that standing on his own two feet would have given him. He had never forgiven Mother for being right.

She had lain in this room, in this very bed, with her ailing heart and flaying tongue. Even silenced by the clutching pain in her chest, she had forced him to read in her every withering glance the depths of his worthlessness.

It took every shred of willpower he could muster to find a little studio apartment on the outskirts and to announce he was going to remain there. After three years, he hoped he might have broken free of Mother. But after the debacle of Elinor's second novel there was no way he could stay in Atlanta—and no place to go but home.

For despite her social whirl, her galas and committee meetings, Elinor had found time to finish *The Ceremony of Innocence*—their novel as he still thought of it—and it had been duly published to unexpectedly good reviews. Carroll was thrilled for her and ecstatic when a copy was delivered to his apartment. He tore open the package and thumbed the brightly jacketed volume searching for the dedication, reliving in his mind the hours they had pored over it together, their intimate discussions, their joint labors.

What slapped him in the face was: "To my devoted husband, Jefferson Davis MacGowan, who backed me every step of the way." There was no mention of him whatsoever. He, who had lavished unstinting encouragement on the woman, as well as creating the novel's very plot structure.

In a frenzy of jealousy, Goslin called or wrote Elinor daily, but received no reply. In his torment, he conceived the idea that if Elinor were to be cast out by her friends and family, she would turn to him as her savior, grateful for his love and devotion, and their life could continue together as he yearned for it to. Goslin lashed out indiscriminately, in a confused storm of emotions throughout the following months—his motives an equal mix of his need for Elinor's love and his desire for revenge—spewing out an endless stream of letters denouncing her: to instructors at the university, to her parents, to influential friends of the MacGowan family, and, finally, to Jefferson.

Jefferson called one day and lit into him in a frenzy. "You stupid little bastard," he shouted into the receiver. "Are you crazy? Elinor takes you in out of pity, and you repay her by spreading lies, trying to ruin her good name. You fell for a woman nearly old enough to be your mother, and now you're trying to parlay that into a ridiculous tale of a love affair."

Appalled, Carroll held the phone away from his ear as Jefferson raved on. "I've kept all the letters you've written me, you silly son of a bitch—and all the ones you've sent here to Elinor, and her parents, and the chairman of my board of directors, and everyone else whose mind you've tried to poison. I want you to know they all came directly to me with your rubbish. I've never seen Elinor so distraught. I want you to understand that if I get one more of these filthy things, I'm going to take the whole pack to my lawyer and have him sue the pants off you for libel and defamation of character, harassment, and any other charge he can dream up."

He stopped for a moment, panting for breath. "And if that doesn't stop you," he rasped, "I'll kill you. I swear I'll find you wherever you are and kill you myself."

Young Carroll, not one to seek physical confrontations even with his peers, never wrote another letter to Jefferson or to Elinor at her home address.

Goslin knew then that he was doomed to return to Boston and Mother. He had gone back briefly after his first holiday visit, then had wrenched himself away from her again and had physically moved to Atlanta to be near Elinor. But the three years in the little apartment, nourished on fragments of unfinished stories and scraps of Elinor's attention, culminating in her perfidy in the book's dedication, marked the final flickering of his strength and the utmost limit of his powers to resist Mother's will. So go back he did, to a woman who despised him, but who at least fiercely wanted and needed him.

Mired in a slough of despair, Goslin allowed his life to be submerged in his mother's. She owned the house, she bought the car—which she insisted on driving, Carroll riding docilely at her side—in her own name, and kept everything down to the utilities and cleaning bills in her maiden name and under her tight supervision. Carroll too, she gathered back under her control. She was a proud woman, and her pride had been badly wounded by his desertion of her for Elinor. She took her revenge leisurely, in tiny, poisoned doses, measured out every minute of every day.

"Why don't you get out more?" she would needle him, knowing she was setting a double-ended trap. "You're the laziest fellow I've ever seen."

And each time, he rose to the bait. "When I tell you I want to go out, you insist you need me here. When I'm here, you want me to go out." And each time his voice sounded shrill and petulant in his own ears, a little boy unable to take charge of his own life.

The truth was, Carroll was afraid, and with good reason. The years away from home had been his youngest and strongest, most filled with hope. But even then he hadn't made his own way. He dabbled at his writing and took courses at a community college near Atlanta. On occasion, he had taken money from Elinor, and always, he relied on the monthly check that Mother had faithfully sent him, despite—or perhaps because of—her wrath at his abandonment. She sent the checks like clockwork, with the certainty that in the long run, Carroll's increasing dependence would be all the more binding. She dared not provoke him to open rebellion—where would she be if he were actually to break free, to stand on his own two feet? There was no love to bind them, but fear sufficed.

Thus Carroll Goslin passed from youth to middle age, settled in to be Mother's companion and dogsbody; trapped, in reality, by his own inertia.

One day, when he happened to collect the mail just before

Mother swooped down on it first, he spotted a heavy, cream envelope addressed in that familiar hand. For a second his chest constricted, then, as Mother called on her way, "Has the mail come?" he'd thrust it inside his shirt, handed her the remainder, and dashed up to his room.

"You naughty Boy!" The words hit him like a splash of cold water. Elinor plunged in as though no time at all had passed, no threats, no years of frigid silence. *"You gave me such a fright, and you made Jefferson so angry! You can't imagine what it was like here! But nobody tells me what to do, and when he said I wasn't to write to you anymore, I wasn't going to be bullied!*

I've been thinking of our wonderful time as students, and how we spent those long nights …

And so I've gone and gotten my own private post box! Jefferson isn't the only one who can play at this, you know, and I'm so hoping that you'll remember your little Evie and write me a few lines. I'm so lonesome way down here …"

There was much, much more, but Goslin put down the letter, saving it to dole out in measured—treasured—doses, and experienced a joy he hadn't known in over a decade. He blocked out all thoughts of the painful past, refused to dwell on why she might have chosen this particular time to write.

That very afternoon he made arrangements for his own private box at the nearby Milk Street post office, taking it out "for his elderly mother" in her name and using her maiden name as his own surname as the designated key holder. Strolling back home, the young couples passing by carrying blankets and coolers—no doubt on their way stake out places for an evening Esplanade concert—gave him a feeling of camaraderie rather than underscoring the bleakness of his own existence, as such scenes usually did. He walked along under the great trees of the Commonwealth Avenue mall, spinning plans for the old townhouse.

Finally, he would reap some pleasure from Mother's money; he and Elinor would throw open the curtained windows to the sun, buy new furniture, formal and splendid, and there would be gracious dinners in the old dining room. He closed his eyes, his yearning so intense that he could smell the savory roast and the hot wax from the candelabra.

Goslin turned and continued back to the Common, then sat down on a wooden bench under the shadow of the mariner's statue looking across the avenue to the Public Garden. He basked in the warmth, the scents, the sounds. There was still time, he marveled. After a period of time to get reacquainted, he would ask Elinor to marry him—and she would say yes. He smiled at a young woman walking a small shaggy dog and was surprised to see her smile in return. She walked on past, leaving a trace of lavender scent in her wake. Goslin took a deep breath of the warm, perfumed air. Why, so many things were possible in this new world where Elinor had sought him out again and where young people were so friendly.

The letter brought him not only rekindled hope, but the courage to act.

Ill she might be, but Mother never believed she could die; never believed that God wouldn't make an exception for her. She must have been even more disbelieving, he mused, rubbing his hands together in the darkness, when a few nights later he had moved her nitroglycerin tablets just out of reach and gone for a long walk through the Common. The house was silent when he returned. It was silent the next morning when he called the family physician, and had remained blessedly silent ever since.

Mother would have won in the end, had he not now had a bright future to look forward to. When the will was read, Goslin learned that while Mother had left him the house and all of her money for his lifetime use, they had been tied up in a trust. The money was to be doled out—generously, he had to admit—but on Mother's terms. If he ever moved out of the house he would forfeit the inheritance altogether. Neither could he sell the house, and, when he died, everything was to go to an obscure nature society—unless he was married. Mother—who had hated all outdoors, and who'd thought him far beyond romance.

The Carroll she had known was too weak and fearful to refuse her largesse; to be able to strike out on his own and to endure life in whatever shabby apartment a fifty-three-year-old man with a librarian's part-time salary could afford. Mother thought she had trapped him neatly, keeping him dependent upon her money and the comforts of the familiar old house while she was alive, then chaining him to her after her death, playing the links on out into the future to the end of his days.

He had gotten rid of the bulk of her furniture and personal effects directly after the funeral, and kept her portrait as a trophy of his triumph.

But he had been stupid tonight. It didn't really upset him that the Colewell woman was dead. She deserved to die as much as the others, all the greedy women who valued their money and comfort over love and companionship. But he had made such a botch of his plan; it was all to do over again.

The boy was a problem. He had nearly come apart when he'd gone down to fetch him and found him escaped. He had to take the chance that Eric couldn't find this house again—there was no reason that he should be able to. The lengthy drive through the North Shore yesterday would have put him off the track, would buy time for him to finish his business with the daughter. He'd gathered up the remnants of discarded cord he'd found by the Dumpster and, to be safe, he would move his car to a different location for a few days.

He had been too hasty tonight—it was a certainty that Gwendolyn would be watched now. He would not act rashly again. The woman had to die, and once she was safely dead, he would take his chances with whatever happened next.

CHAPTER THIRTEEN

By eleven Saturday morning rain was falling in a fine, steady drizzle, nearly obliterating the brown stains on the patio flagstones, blurring their spattered outlines on the wooden picnic table and bench. There was a silvery sheen to the sky as the sun tried to burn through the clouds, but the air remained hot and muggy. Gwendolyn and Thibodeau stood inside the confines of the steaming garage, examining the remaining boxes.

"Only eight more to go," said Gwendolyn optimistically. "Let's pull out the relevant stuff and bring it into the house to read. It'll be safer inside. I guess I mean that *I'll* feel safer inside," she amended. "We can sort the weird stuff out pretty quickly. I put that last letter in my desk yesterday before I left to make the funeral arrangements."

"Okay. Somewhere she's got to have put down a name or an address or taken a photo. Nobody's totally anonymous, and they both wrote so much so often, that one of them was bound to have gotten careless."

Gwendolyn handed Thibodeau an empty box. "Here, put whatever you find in this. We should be able to finish up this afternoon. I'll spend the rest of the weekend reading and sorting it."

"Not much," said Thibodeau after they had worked in silence for half an hour. "Books, photos. I pulled out a few shots of various men, but I don't see anything promising. That reminds me. I've arranged for the police artist to be downtown at two. I want Eric to work with him on a composite sketch. Then I want him to go through some mug shots. I doubt this guy has any priors—sounds more like a nutcase with a personal grudge—but we have to try. I'll bring Eric back afterward. You won't be alone; a policewoman's been assigned to stay here for a few days. She's coming later this afternoon."

"I'll give Eric till noon and then go roust him out. He was still out cold when you came, and I didn't have the heart to wake him."

Thibodeau pulled open another box. "Books," he said. He examined each volume and then piled it on one of the stacks and went on to the next box. "What was your mother's book called?"

"*The Ceremony of Innocence.* It must sound crazy that I couldn't bear to keep one, but it was just too highly charged. It's too bad she had to die before I could think about it. Our family's like radioactive waste; there's a half-life to wait through before anything's touchable—like Strontium-90. Unfortunately, the wait is longer than our natural lives …"

Thibodeau was silent. He found nothing appropriate or comforting to say. They worked on, listening to the hiss of the rain on the warm concrete.

"Well," said Gwendolyn, sitting back on her heels, holding up a handful of letters, "I think I've hit the mother lode. The fire-and-brimstone stuff, like yesterday's. They read like something out of Revelations or Apocalypse. Whoever he was, it sounds like he and Mother were awfully close and then something went very, very wrong. He seems to be going crazy. Gwendolyn thrust the letters aside abruptly and stood up. "I'm going in to check on Eric. I can't take too much of this at once. Would you like a cup of coffee? Something cold? Iced tea?"

"Iced tea would be fine," Thibodeau, said, digging into another box.

Gwendolyn was gone briefly, returning with two tall glasses. "I found some old clothes of mine for Eric. He says he isn't hungry, so I told him to come out when he's dressed and have his tea with us."

They sipped tea for a few minutes and then went back to the boxes. "Look at this, Gwen, there are several smaller boxes in this carton. I thought it was just typewriter paper, but it's the original manuscript of *The Ceremony of Innocence*. And here's another. This one's called *The Lying Days of Youth*."

"Let me see." She thumbed the thick stack. "There's 243 pages of it, but it breaks off midchapter. It must be the one she was working on when she stopped writing altogether. I wonder what it's about. Interesting—she's dated the first page of each chapter in pencil, just like she did the letters. Chapter one starts on December 6, 1951, and the unfinished chapter is dated May 29, 1954. I guess I've got my night's reading cut out for me."

She broke off as Eric came up with his glass of iced tea. The boy's thin face was still pinched, but he seemed to have gained more substance in a pair of Gwendolyn's old sweatpants and a plaid, cotton short-sleeved shirt.

"How're you holding up, Eric?" asked Thibodeau, his words abrupt, but his voice kind.

Eric narrowed his eyes and then accepted the man's words at face value.

"Very well, sir." He hesitated. "What will happen now? Will I be sent back to England?"

Gwendolyn glanced at Thibodeau. "I'm afraid I hadn't even thought about that, Eric. Do you have any other relatives back in England? We should contact them as soon as possible so that they can make arrangements for your mother." She looked at the boy, hesitating to be more specific, but Eric didn't show any sign of distress.

"Only my aunt Glynnis, Mother's older sister. She lives in London, but we rarely see her. I don't know her address, but her name is Glynnis Colewell. Mother would have her name in her address book, if she brought it with her. My father may have relatives here, but mother never mentioned any. I've never even seen a photograph of him."

Gwendolyn looked uncomfortably at Thibodeau, who shook his head slightly. Turning to the boy he said, "I'll find your aunt, Eric, and notify her about your mother."

"You'll stay here, of course," Gwendolyn found herself saying. "At least until we decide what to do. Would you like anything to eat yet?"

He shook his head. "I don't eat very much," he said, his voice reverting from that of a composed young man to a childish whine. "Is there any hot tea?" he asked. He held the plastic glass out in front of him with both hands, like a beggar seeking alms.

"Well, you've seen where the kitchen is. The kettle's on the stove, and the teabags and mugs are on the counter by the stove. You can help yourself to anything there, or wait a bit until I fix lunch. We'll be working here for at least another half hour or forty-five minutes, but you can come sit with us, if you like. I think you'll feel better if you eat something, though, because you're going to have to go downtown in a while to look at some photographs."

Eric was surprised that he wasn't going to be coaxed into eating. Heretofore, a good portion of his daily routine involved his refusal of a suggested course of action and his mother's wheedling and coaxing him into finally performing it. As Gwendolyn turned back to her task, it suddenly dawned on him that he wouldn't get breakfast at all unless he took the initiative. Realizing simultaneously that he was, indeed, very hungry, he set off to the kitchen to feed himself.

"Poor kid," nodded Thibodeau toward his retreating back. "Still, he kind of makes you want to smack him."

"I know what you mean," agreed Gwendolyn. "I think his bad leg is the least of his disabilities. It wouldn't surprise me if this is the first time he's ever had to get his own breakfast. Yesterday morning, Monica was telling me about all his medication, but he seemed to get through his ordeal without it, and when I asked him about it this morning, he told me he didn't really need all that stuff, that he knew it made his mother feel better to give it to him. I felt a little mean, just now," Gwendolyn confessed, "but after all ..."

"Are you going to tell him that he's your half brother? I've been thinking you should consider it pretty carefully first. That's why I nodded at you."

"Thanks, but I wasn't going to say anything now, anyway. I'm not sure what good it would do, and it could do a lot of harm."

‡   ‡   ‡

Carroll Goslin was out and about as soon as the stores were open Saturday morning. He decided not to retrieve his car, but to use public transportation for his various errands. He walked down Charles Street to the T station and rode the two stops to Central Square, where he bought a number of items at an Army surplus store. He next visited a used-clothing shop and a hardware store, putting his assorted purchases into a sturdy new canvas duffel bag.

He walked back toward the subway station, oblivious to the penetrating rain. His hat turned aside most of the moisture from his face, and the long, black coat was nearly waterproof. He was invisible to the Hispanic women herding broods of children, the grizzle-chinned winos, and gaggles of loud teenagers hurrying along the sidewalks or huddling under store awnings.

He stepped into the subway entrance and looked around cautiously before descending into its depths. He took an inbound train to Park Square, changed to a trolley, and exited at Copley Square. Goslin then spent several hours in the Boston Public Library reference area, poring over the *Dun & Bradstreet* volumes, and xeroxing the Art and Framing pages in the Yellow Pages. Before leaving the library at noon, he went down to the fiction section but could find no catalogue listing under "Dulac, Evelyn."

The house was very quiet with Thibodeau and Eric gone. Gwendolyn retreated to her bedroom on the third floor, laying out letters and papers on the floor, trying to determine some logical way to put them in order. The room was large and airy, its corner location over the back of the house affording pleasant cross-ventilation as well as privacy. The floor was exposed, its polished hardwood highlighted by two colorful woven throw rugs. Next to the queen-sized bed was a night table with a telephone and small fan, and beside that, next to the door, a bookcase stocked with whatever books currently interested her. Gwendolyn kept the bulk of her library downstairs but had discovered she was unable to sleep in an entirely bookless room.

A gable thrust out over the back of the house, and here Gwendolyn had arranged a recliner, another small table, and a reading light. Two tiers of deep shelving, running along the entire wall to the left of the door, held a large television and two VCRs, visible from both the bed and the recliner, and dozens of cassette boxes. When not reading, Gwendolyn's passion was taping and watching selected series of old detective TV shows, black-and-white classics, and old British comedies.

Two original photographs hung on either side of the bed; a Berenice Abbott portrait of James Joyce that Gwendolyn had purchased in a collection for her store, and a 1908 view of St. Paul's Cathedral by Alvin Langdon Coburn, a bit of serendipity she had bought for five dollars in a junk shop. On top of the bookcase was a small, gold double frame, with photographs of her parents as children. Young Jefferson, about ten, wore short pants, one black stocking torn loose from its moorings to reveal a bare knee, an arm around a spotted hound he once told her was named Scout. His cap was pushed back to one side of his head giving him a rakish, mischievous air.

Elinor had been captured when she was about seven or eight. The photo had been hand-tinted in soft colors that still held their glow. The little girl wore a wide-brimmed straw hat with a huge flower and leaned her elbow on the arm of a wicker chair, her tilted head propped on her bent wrist. In her other hand she held a little folded parasol. Her weight rested on one leg, the other knee crossed, her foot resting on its toes, looking quite Victorian in her high-buttoned boots. Her pink cheeks matched the rosy sash tied about the waist of her white dress, an enchanting mixture of innocent and flirt.

Gwendolyn put on a tape of *The Third Man* and began to sort the papers into piles. She started with the ones she had brought in Sunday evening. Most were written in the nonsense code and dated at the top by her mother. Idly, Gwendolyn opened an envelope that didn't seem to fit in.

"Knowing that you like to have some props when you play to an audience, here is something for you to tear up this May 24 like you tore up the letter last year from the one from whom you still take sustenance.

"Be violent in tearing it up so that externally you can convey emotion, an element that is unknown to you internally.

"Much luck for another 24 years of sponging.*

'sponge: …' 2. Colloq. To get a living, a meal, etc. meanly at the expense of another or by imposition. To get without cost in a mean, cringing, or underhand way."

"My God!" Gwendolyn cried aloud, throwing the letter away from her. To write a letter like that—to receive a letter like that—and then to *keep* it. She shuddered.

She recognized the bold, sloping letters and May 24th had been her parents' anniversary. The letter was postmarked Atlanta. This hadn't been sent by the man who sent the others, but by her father. She got up from the floor and went to the bookcase. She picked up the frame and studied the photographs again. The mischievous little boy and the flirtatious little girl. The boy turned vicious? The coquette a hollow shell? Some terrible scene had to have taken place the previous year to cause her father to nurse such bitterness, waiting and hating for 364 days, counting the hours until he could send this piece of vitriol to his wife on their next anniversary. That was the year she and her father had gone fishing so often, she remembered now. While they were standing in the rippling trout streams was he mentally composing this? Had they then all sat down together as a family that night of the twenty-fourth? Had they perhaps gone out to one of the dinners that Gwendolyn so dreaded at the Golf Club and had another scene in public? She couldn't for the life of her remember. But shouldn't that kind of hatred leave a visible mark, like a poisonous slug trailing a viscous ribbon of bitterness and malice across the years?

Gwendolyn picked up another group of envelopes from the original sender. Many of these bore slightly later dates, and it was obvious as they progressed that whatever her mother and their author had shared, had vanished completely; the same bitterness and hatred her father had poured into his short note had inspired this writer, too.

They began with hints and innuendoes and grew stronger over time. "The enclosed is a startling offer," one began. "The interesting part is—some don't want freedom. Unexplained tension is difficult to overcome where the cause is kept secret—or maybe not consciously known. Relax."

A full-page newspaper ad was enclosed: "How to Defend Yourself Against the HUMAN PARASITES Who Want to Rule Your Life!" Promising a new philosophy that would allow the reader to "take command of his life" and rid himself of those who love aggressively, with guilt and dominance. Examples had been underlined and an arrow drawn to the category "The Love Dominator," the "woman who first 'loves' you and then destroys you!"

The earlier letters were addressed by hand, then changed to the type that characterized the latest envelopes Elinor had received in Boston, growing more vicious and incoherent—and then suddenly ceased.

Gwendolyn's cheeks burned with shame and humiliation as she absorbed the naked anger on the pages, as though the words were aimed at her directly. She shook herself awake from a near hypnotic state and realized that her concentration had been so intense that she had put herself in her mother's place. She felt demeaned, abased; worse, she felt that she deserved the abuse.

Mechanically, Gwendolyn picked up another letter beginning, "Heed this. You think you are successful, talented, destined for success. But you are consummately wrong. You are an empty vessel, cold, lying, a traitor to those who loved you and helped you. Perhaps there is still time to seek treatment for the disease that consumes you, and become again, if you ever were, a caring, feeling human being."

Four pages of single-spaced type of this nature accompanied a long scientific piece on schizophrenia from the *New York Times Magazine.* Gwendolyn skimmed through the others. It seemed that any piece on deviant behavior in every major newspaper or magazine published on the Eastern seaboard had been clipped, with an eye to pointing out some new, unwholesome facet of Elinor's personality. What did that say about the eye of the beholder?

Wedged into one of the letters was a four-by-five-inch brown photographic sleeve, open at one end. Gwendolyn slipped out a packet of photographs and was startled to see her mother in a plaid skirt and white blouse, head thrown back in a mock movie-star pose, knee bent, the hem of her skirt held up between her thumb and forefinger, hand held behind her cocked head. Gwendolyn knew the emotion was genuine, and she could hear Elinor's hearty, spontaneous laugh echo in the empty room. When had she last heard her mother laugh like that? She must have been very small, but there had once been a time when the sound of her mother's open laugh could ignite her own childish joy.

When had the joy fled? Why? Once her parents had laughed together, sitting in the living room, listening to records, just enjoying each other's company or letting her snuggle in between them. When she was very small, maybe three or four, she remembered, her mother would play the piano while her father walked up and down the room with Gwendolyn over his shoulder until she was fast asleep. Try as she would to stay awake, she would find herself in her bed the next morning, never remembering being tucked in. That was before the long nights began when she lay awake alone for hours, listening to the angry voices that never seemed to stop. A year ago, on a visit to Copley Court, Gwendolyn had told her mother how much she had enjoyed her piano playing, pointing out to her that there was a baby grand downstairs in the library. Elinor had looked out of the window and murmured, "I got over that …"

Gwendolyn shook her head and fanned the photographs. There were twelve in all: three shots of her mother clowning for the camera, and three more of her holding notebooks in front of a stone building on what looked like a college campus. There were two full-length pictures of a young man in his early twenties also holding a notebook and books in front of the same building.

He was wearing a jacket and slacks and a dark tie. The last four had been taken by a third person. They were of her mother and the young man. With her mother for comparison, it was obvious that the man was tall, well over six feet. She remembered Eric's description of the photo in her mother's book. She could see what he meant now. With a little makeup and exaggeration of the features, his face would look bizarre, Karloffian; here, beaming at the camera, the face was simply oversized, that of a large, pale, good-natured young man.

Gwendolyn took one of the snaps of her mother and the man and propped it up against a leg of the recliner so that she could study it as she worked. The two made a pleasant-looking couple. Her mother, obviously the older of the two, was happy, vibrant, her face caught in an openness that was unfamiliar to Gwendolyn. Typically, her mother focused her attention on the camera, while the young man, obviously smitten, gazed at her mother. She studied the buildings in the background of the other photos. These could well have been taken that summer when her mother was in New York at Columbia, but who was the man? She turned over each snapshot, but there were no dates, no notation of location or identity. Gwendolyn tried to think back to that time. Had her mother ever mentioned a friend? All she could remember was that her father had been upset the whole time that Elinor had stayed in New York.

"My pencil box!" she exclaimed. She remembered as if she held it in her hands now—a tooled leather pencil box—well, maybe it hadn't been real leather, but it had raised designs of little squirrels and acorns and oak leaf garlands, and she distinctly remembered convincing her best friend, Weezie Markham, that it was real, tooled leather.

The box was a rich, saddle-leather brown, sleek as pony hide to her touch. It had contained a dozen brightly colored wooden pencils, each with her name stamped on it in gold; a soft, blushing Pink Pearl eraser; and two wooden penholders with an assortment of pen nibs. There were intriguing little compartments for paper clips, gummed labels, and binder hole stickum-things. Gwendolyn had especially prized a highly varnished six-inch ruler with a metal edge because with it she could finally make pen lines without the ink running under and blotting the paper.

Someone had given it to her one Christmas when she was in second grade. Gwendolyn closed her eyes and tried to picture the moment. Her mother had been there, but it wasn't Mother who had given it to her. Someone tall had reached down to hand it to her; she could see his large, white hands holding the present. Her mother had seemed unusually anxious and nudged her sharply. "Darling," she had prompted Gwendolyn, "say, 'Thank you,' to"—to whom?

She loved that box so much that she hadn't taken it out often—except to use the ruler—and would just marvel at the pencils and the tiny compartments. Each time she would return it carefully to her desk drawer to keep it new and clean. Then one day mother had come to her and told her that she must give it back, that there were some things she had to give back to a friend, and the pencil box was one of them. Gwendolyn had thought it was silly to give back pencils that already had her name on them—who else would want them?—but her mother had insisted, and Gwendolyn, after slipping out the little ruler, had surrendered the box. The only other thing that she could recall was her mother kissing her perfunctorily and whispering in a voice of forced camaraderie, "This will just be our little secret, won't it, Gwennie?" Funny, how both mother and father called her "Gwennie" when they were making her an accomplice to some little secret one wanted to keep from the other. *My "tail-in-the-crack" nickname*, she thought ruefully.

By three o'clock, Gwendolyn had sorted several distinct piles of material. There were the early letters with and without envelopes that she had found Sunday; there were those from the same author that went from handwritten to typed, with their spectrum of violent emotions; there were the undated photos; and finally, the daunting manuscripts of *The Ceremony of Innocence* and *The Lying Days of Youth*.

Having had her fill of the ghastly letters, Gwendolyn decided to tackle the book. It made her queasy to think about reading her mother's manuscripts, but there was no way around it. She picked up the unfinished pages, thinking they might be more likely to yield a clue to her mother's behavior than the already published *Innocence*. She read diligently for a bit, then skipped ahead to see if her expectations proved to be true.

Chapter 9

"Scott, you are such a silly boy. Of course I love you, My Darling, but you never truly believed, did you, that ours was more than a summer romance? It was mad, it was wonderful—but leave my home? Leave my precious child? Would you have me break my poor husband's heart? To run away and live with you in your tiny— although charming, My Love—attic in Greenwich Village is quite out of the question. Surely you see the folly of it all?"

"Oh Rebecca, my own Dear Heart. I am not a silly boy, I am a

man, a man who adores you and who can make you happy, if you will but let me. You promised me our ages made no difference to you! You gave me your pledge that you would be mine! You swore you would renounce your husband, your daughter, life here in Richmond— everything—to come with me, to be my soul mate, my companion, my love. Yes, I am young, but I have my life ahead of me. I have my work. I know I have great books within me, Rebecca, but I need you by my side to give them birth."

Poor Scott, thought Gwendolyn, setting the heavy manuscript down on the bed beside her. Too bad he hadn't met Monica instead. He could be fishing those sparkling English streams and tramping those heathered heaths. And she could be alive.

Instead, Scott was whining through 200-odd unrequited pages of *The Lying Days of Youth*, trying to win the faithless Rebecca. Most of the lying, it appeared to Gwendolyn, was being done by Rebecca, not the youth. Rebecca swept through the novel, page after florid page, regal, gracious, stamping her tiny foot, both literally and figuratively, during whatever moments Scott wasn't kissing it, either literally or figuratively. Gwendolyn could imagine her mother at the typewriter, fingers itching to type "Scarlett" and forced to settle for "Rebecca."

Well, poor maundering Scott was no Rhett Butler either. Gwendolyn wondered if his prototype had gotten a glimpse of these pages. If so, it might well have been "Scott" who put quits to her mother's getting this one published. And, if Scott was anything of the man he kept insisting he was in his turgid speeches, he might have worked up one hopping great rage against the woman who used his sacred love as fodder for her profane romance novel.

A young man. A much younger man. Had she ever met him if he had, indeed, been real? If only she could visualize the tall man reaching down to hand her the gift that Christmas. "Darling, say, 'Thank you' to—?" It was as far as she could go each time she played the scene over in her mind.

She needed to rest. Just a little nap … She leaned back against the bed and closed her eyes, letting her mind float.

She was dressed to the nines, on display at one of her parents' parties, carrying a plate of canapés around to the guests. It must have been a Christmas party, because she was wearing her red velvet dress with the bright-green sash. Green velvet bows tied off the plaits that her mother had braided so tightly that her temples ached. Her mother came up to her and told her to put down the tray. She led Gwendolyn into the library where a tall, pale man was standing self-consciously, holding out a package tied in silver paper.

Chapter Fourteen

The front doorbell buzzer wired into her bedroom rang, and Gwendolyn's eyes snapped open. She glanced at the clock on her bedside table. Four thirty ... she'd napped much longer than she'd planned.

It was the police officer that Thibodeau had promised to have assigned to her. Patricia Hanley, to Gwendolyn's great relief, turned out to be a polite, taciturn woman in her midthirties. Gwendolyn gave her the room next to Eric's, wondering how such an assignment would be handled if the threatened subject lived in a studio apartment ... She had shown officer Hanley the kitchen and living room and offered her the run of the house when Hanley, who had merely murmured and nodded till then, spoke up.

"And where're your quarters?"

Gwendolyn led her up the front stairway to the third floor and onto an octagonal landing, pointing out, "These doors opening off here—it's kind of confusing at first—go to the back stairway, kitchen, bath, and office. Well, it's an office in name only; I store my shop records in there and work in the living room. My bedroom's at the end of this hallway down in back. I like it secluded. Very little noise, no neighbors."

As they walked down toward the bedroom, Gwendolyn opened a door revealing a modern kitchen. "I'm so glad I had the good sense to leave this upstairs kitchen intact," she said. "The previous owner made ends meet by illegally renting single rooms to four extra tenants, and he'd jerry-rigged extra kitchen areas for them, two on the second floor and this one. When I started to remodel the house, I had the kitchens on the second floor removed and this one renovated for my tenants.

"Luckily, things got better at my store, and I no longer had to have tenants. I wanted the whole place for myself, so I staked out the third floor and kept the kitchen for a separate suite. If I need to, I can stay up here in my own private world as long as the food holds out."

"Hmmmm," was Hanley's only comment.

Thibodeau had returned at six thirty with a cranky Eric, tired and irritable from fruitlessly poring over volumes of mug shots in the sweltering station house.

"I've got a picture for you, Eric," said Gwendolyn, remembering her find. "I'll be right back."

"That's the man!" cried Eric as soon as she handed him the photographs. "And that one is like the one of the man and the woman in the book. I think he's heavier now, and of course he's older. The man I was with had hair that was going gray."

"Great, Eric," said Thibodeau. "Can I use the phone, Gwen? I'll have a car take this downtown directly and get it out with a

BOLO—'Be on the lookout for.' Without a name, we can't put out an APB, but we can get word to the surrounding towns and on the air with the composite shot. That may stir up something. Somebody's got to know the guy by sight if he lives in the area."

Eric's crankiness was forgotten as he told Gwendolyn about his afternoon, the words tumbling out. "And I talked with the police artist. I described the man, and we picked out features from this kit—it had all kinds of noses and ears and things—and I think it looked pretty much like him when we finished. It wasn't quite *exactly* him, you know, but I thought it was awfully close."

"Don't sell yourself short, son," said Thibodeau, back from making his call. "That sketch is being sent out on the wire services and to all the TV stations. It may very well be what will catch your mother's killer."

Eric sat up straighter and rushed on to tell Gwendolyn how he and Thibodeau had tried to find the house where he had been held captive. "Warren and I went to the bus station and tried to walk back the way I came last night. What was the name of that fancy hotel?"

"The Ritz. Yes, Eric and I went back along Arlington Street past the Ritz, but he lost the trail at the intersection of Commonwealth Avenue. He remembered having the Garden on his left, but he seems to have wandered for some time before he became aware of his surroundings. From his description of the alley, he could have been anywhere in any one of a hundred narrow side streets in any one of a hundred brick buildings."

"And I was blindfolded going in and out, don't forget, and it was either dark or raining both times."

"You did a fine job escaping from the guy," said Thibodeau as

Gwendolyn set out macaroni and cheese dinners for them. "You'd better believe that not everyone could have done that."

As they were finishing supper, the doorbell rang and Thibodeau handed over the photos to an officer with instructions to have them processed and distributed. He asked Pat Hanley to take Eric outside so that he could talk with Gwendolyn.

"I think whoever sent those letters could be the killer, Gwen," he said when they were alone. "And he may well be the man in the pictures. I wish we had an ID on him."

"I just can't remember if I ever met him. I don't recognize the man in the photo. I keep going over being introduced to Mother's friend but haven't had any success with a name. I think that young man and the subject of her unfinished manuscript tie in too."

"How so?"

"I went through a good deal of it this afternoon, and the heroine, Rebecca, meets this young fellow while they're away at a summer writer's conference. The book's set in the Midwest, but it follows just the way she lived in New York when she took those courses at Columbia, and if she really used their own experiences as a model, she made a complete fool of him."

"What happened?" pursued Thibodeau.

"Naturally, they have an affair that summer at the conference. Then the boy comes to Richmond to visit her. In fact, he moves away from home and takes an apartment there in Richmond. She's married, of course—it's a pretty stock melodrama. For a couple of years he waits, believing that she's making plans to leave her family and run away with him. He's dreaming of their future life together, while she's just flattered by the younger man's attention and is using him to make her husband jealous. It must have been awful for the fellow—if he ever found out—that she was working away on her own novel and exploiting his emotions. By anyone's standards, the book was going along well, if you like that kind of writing—and since her first book had been successful, the only reason I can think of for her stopping would be some kind of drastic intervention—maybe by the guy himself."

"Or your father—ah, her husband," amended Thibodeau. "If she'd been using this young guy to make him jealous, then other people would have known about him too, and the book would have made your father look like a fool and a cuckold. Either one of them could have felt pretty violently about it."

"Haven't they discovered anything from Monica's murder?" asked Gwendolyn.

"No. In spite of the butchery, there wasn't any hard information. He didn't panic and drop his knife, and he didn't touch anything or leave prints. There might have been some footprints if the rain hadn't been so heavy, but the ground had been pretty dry for the last few weeks and wouldn't have taken a very traceable impression, anyway. Your street is paved and kept clean, no mud to pick up a tire print. We questioned Eric pretty thoroughly, but he doesn't know anything about cars, and you can't blame the poor kid for not sticking around to memorize the license plate once he'd escaped. He says the car was green, and it had four doors, because he got out of a back one. That would narrow it down to about ten thousand or so green, four-door cars in the greater Boston area."

He gathered up a stack of dishes and took them to the sink. "Tomorrow's Sunday, but we'll have to keep working." Without thinking, he squirted some Ivory into the sink and turned on the hot water. He noticed Gwendolyn smiling at him and grinned sheepishly. "Habit," he said. "And I think better when I'm doing something."

"I want to try a different tack tomorrow," he continued as he washed and rinsed. "We've been concentrating on your mother's letters, but I want to pull your father's letters too. Your mother and her fellow may never have used each other's real names. Your father might have been more direct. Nobody suffers that long in silence, and I'll bet he blew off steam to somebody. Maybe he did it on paper, since he was obsessed with putting everything down and saving it. I'd get Albano here, but you know your mother better than anyone else, and I don't think I have to know your father too well to spot a reference to a lover."

"I hadn't thought of my father's side, but you're right," said Gwendolyn, picking up a red-checked dish towel. "He was vicious to Mother in one note that I found, and he may have confided to someone else. Keep an eye out for the name Langdon. Dad and Tom Langdon were buddies from way back. Tom moved to Denver years ago, but they always kept in touch. And Rachel MacGowan, his sister. She and Mother hated one another, and she would have been happy to rake her over the coals."

"Will do. And maybe you'll remember some other friend of the family or someone that you saw with your mother that might be a lead. If we can just get a name, we can get on his trail. The big question now is whether the guy's had enough, or whether he's a total nut case and will be coming back for you, too. It's something we have to consider."

"Indeed …"

"Cheer up, Gwen. We'll get on with it in the morning. Walk me to the car?" Thibodeau pushed open the screen and stepped out onto the patio.

"This is all scary," said Gwendolyn, "but it's been a revelation to me, too. I'd always been aware of Dad's women; after all, they were pretty visible, but I really don't recall Mother and anybody. She was always raving on at my father about his affairs and so on, and it never crossed my mind that she might have had something on the side, too. It's certainly possible, though. They were both always going out for "committee meetings" and so forth, so they could have been doing most anything. Do you suppose all that rage was just a clever smokescreen? A diversionary tactic? Who were they, Warren? Who was I, for that matter—Mother's Pink Spider? Dad's Waiter for the Tiger? Sometimes I've thought I was the White Bird."

"What white bird is that, Gwen?" asked Thibodeau, opening the car door.

"I'm sure you've seen them on the *Geographic* specials, those cleaner birds darting in to pick tidbits out of the croc's teeth? I spent my life in the jaws of crocodiles."

CHAPTER FIFTEEN

I
t was going on 11:30. Gwendolyn found she was unable to get
to sleep after her conversation with Thibodeau and decided
to go see whether either Pat Hanley or Eric would join her for
some tea or cocoa. She knocked at Hanley's door first, but she
had already made herself a cup of tea and was ensconced in bed
watching television. She then tapped softly at Eric's door, in case
he was asleep, but she heard the creaking of his bed and his slow
steps coming toward the door.

She softened at the sight of the boy wearing her pajamas and
terrycloth robe like a pup tent, and for the first time was truly
aware that he was now her only living relative, half or not.

"Would you like to come downstairs and have a cup of cocoa
with me?"

He nodded. His shoulder blades poked out like a coat hanger
under the rough terrycloth. "When was the last time you ate?"
Gwendolyn asked. "I was watching you at dinner, and you were
just rearranging your food with your fork. I don't think you ate
three mouthfuls. Maybe a peanut butter and jelly sandwich would
hit the spot. How about it, Eric?"

"I'm not really …" Eric began.

"You ought to be," Gwendolyn interrupted briskly. "We'll look around and see if anything else appeals to you. On second thought, you go on in the living room, and I'll get us a snack. I think we'll be more comfortable there. Wait, I'll come in with you." She settled him on the couch and put a tape of *The Ladykillers* in the VCR.

"Ever seen this one, Eric? It's awfully good."

"No, Miss MacGowan—I mean Gwendolyn—I didn't go to the cinema very often, and we only watched the educational programs on the television. Mother said watching too much was bad for my eyes, but I did sneak back sometimes and watch late-night horror movies after she was asleep sometimes."

"Well, I don't think Alec Guinness will do you irreparable damage. Just relax, and I'll be right back."

Gwendolyn took time to make a giant bowl of buttered popcorn and mugs of cocoa, then heaped a plate with waffle-creme and chocolate chip cookies. When she got back to the living room, Eric was totally engrossed in the movie. Gwendolyn slipped Eric's cocoa and the cookies within his reach and set the bowl of popcorn between them on the sofa. Without taking his eyes off the screen, Eric picked up his mug of cocoa with one hand and a vanilla-creme cookie with the other and began to eat steadily.

In the next hour and a half, Eric drank two more cups of cocoa and in between handfuls of popcorn, cleaned up most of the cookies on the platter. He never took his eyes off the screen, and several times made a ratchety sound in his throat that Gwendolyn realized was laughter. As the film rewound, Eric leaned his head on the arm of the couch and fell into a deep sleep.

Gwendolyn cleared the dishes and then shook the boy partially awake and walked him upstairs to bed.

"I guess I have enough movies to keep you fed while you're here," Gwendolyn laughed as she tucked him in and switched out the light.

Carroll Goslin plucked at the quilted coverlet, turning and smoothing the sheets with precise strokes of his broad palms, his eyes open wide in the blackness. He had extinguished the aquarium lights—they and the humming aerators had lost their power to soothe.

The entire house was silent—none of the tiny crepitations of aged Victorian wood or the whispering wind through tall, uninsulated casements. The opaqued windows that had guarded his privacy in this room over the years were claustrophobic, his bed had become a narrow coffin, the darkness a black shroud closing in.

The veins in his temples throbbed, his breathing grew rapid and shallow until he was dizzy, gasping for precious mouthfuls of air like an eyeless deep-sea creature dragged up out of its depth. Paralyzed in the graveyard blackness, he felt the walls closing in to crush him.

With a stifled cry, Goslin summoned all his will power to reach out and switch on the bedside lamp. He lay supine in the dim circle of yellow light, trembling, panting, his heart pounding in its cage.

His breathing steadied, and he sat up, swathed in his sweat-soaked pajamas. He reached for his robe at the foot of the bed, and swung his feet over the edge, long, flexible toes searching for their slippers. He shuffled downstairs to the kitchen and put a saucepan of milk on to heat. The clock above the stove read 2:17.

He'd gone to bed early, thinking to get a good night's sleep in preparation for the final task. He was tired from the unaccustomed outing earlier—the Saturday crowds—but despite his fatigue he was pleased with his accomplishments, so much so that he now rallied and decided to celebrate with a feast of chicken breasts in cream sauce with grapes and white wine. He laid a place in the dining room at the old mahogany table, and, after preparing and cooking his feast, ate leisurely and with relish. Sated, he went upstairs to his bedroom, changed into clean pajamas, and fell at once into a dreamless sleep.

When he switched on the television set in Mother's room the next morning, Channel 5 was blaring, "And still no leads in the slasher slaying of Monica Colewell. At the time of her death, Mrs. Colewell, a British citizen, was the guest of Gwendolyn MacGowan at her residence in Jamaica Plain." There was the patio, bathed in the white glare of television lights, then the view panned across the beech trees and a section of the yard, lurching disconcertingly as the hand-held camera followed a covered gurney being wheeled to an ambulance.

"This composite picture of the alleged killer was made by a police artist from a description given by Eric Colewell, the nineteen-year-old son of the victim, who in a bizarre chain of events was kidnapped Friday by the man now being sought in the Colewell slaying."

The camera cut to a hideous face, whose bulging eyes, domed forehead, and prognathous jaw lent it such an expression of bestial depravity and deranged abandon as to be virtually unrecognizable to him as Carroll Goslin. Shaken as he was to learn that he was now being actively pursued, Goslin, who had always pictured himself physically as open-faced and sensitive, was primarily outraged that anyone who had ever been a guest in his home—even under duress—should slander him with such an appalling caricature. He continued to watch, mesmerized.

"He is also wanted for questioning in last week's murder of Elinor Buell MacGowan, the mother of Gwendolyn MacGowan, and for the kidnapping of Eric Colewell."

Goslin was stunned by their next shot, a photo of Elinor and himself taken that first summer in New York. His stomach heaved, he felt stripped naked as the voice-over described their photo as "believed to be the alleged killer with his first victim, Elinor MacGowan, taken about 1950."

"This man is armed and extremely dangerous," the newsman continued, obviously relishing the potential danger from the security of his television studio. "If you see this man, do not, I repeat, do not approach him, but call one of the numbers shown below."

Goslin snapped off the set and sat trembling in Mother's armchair. Worse than the shock of the broadcast were her accusing eyes behind him, and her venomous words piercing his being.

"You brought this on yourself, Carly, you know that, don't you? You let that woman make a fool of you, laugh at you, write your life down in black-and-white for the whole world to see. You dragged that miserable affair out for years, and then, when you finally made an end of her, what do you do but go and drag in the other whore and murder her out of blind stupidity. You're as bad as your father. Both killers. Both stupid. If only my Sarah ..."

Goslin hurled himself from the room, for once not waiting until she finished. Sometimes she took hours, just as she had when he was a child. Occasionally, his father would protect him from her vitriol. But Father left not long after Sarah's death, hounded relentlessly by Mother's blame and accusations. Sarah had slipped away that day at the beach while he and Father were playing catch a few yards away. A chance wave, an undertow, and his little sister's life was snuffed out in seconds. Mother blamed the accident on Father and hated Carroll, the image of her tall, quiet husband, for not having been the one to drown. From that day on, however hard he tried to please, Carroll not only failed to replace the effervescent Sarah but remained a constant reminder of her loss.

Just two months after the accident, on his ninth birthday, Carroll waited all afternoon for Father to take him downtown to choose his first bicycle, his promised birthday gift. Father never returned. After a silent dinner, Mother served him a slice of dry cake and a dish of ice cream, but there was no bicycle, no birthday kiss, no "Happy Birthday, Carly"—and she never again mentioned Father.

Mother had all of Father's belongings boxed and taken away—every book, every pipe and ashtray, every photograph—down to the little snapshot on Carroll's dresser. He grieved, for it was the only picture of the two of them together, taken on a rare outing at the Eastern States Exposition over in Springfield. It was the autumn he'd turned six. He wanted a pony ride, and Father asked the proprietor to take the snap. Father, smiling, held the pony's bridle, while he, sitting straight as a little soldier, solemnly clutched the pommel of the western saddle. Carroll ventured to question Mother about his father only once, receiving a painful whipping, but no further explanation.

Stopping by his room to collect the brass key, Carroll made his way to the top floor thinking of that old snapshot. *I feel old*, he thought and then reminded himself, *I am old*. He would be sixty-one years old his next birthday—September 29th, the day Father vanished—and he was very tired.

It was hard to imagine himself aged; hard enough even to imagine himself as an adult, a "grown-up." He had never quite known what that meant or what he was supposed to do once he had achieved that status. As far as Carroll could ever tell, his sole duty was to remain Mother's whipping boy until he died of old age. It wasn't that he had never left home; after Sarah's death it seemed that he was always away. In an effort to rid herself of his presence, Mother had sent him to one boarding school after another, but it never worked out; after a semester or two he would be sent back home, usually preceded by a tactful letter couched in genteel but firm tones, stating that, "Such-and-Such School or Academy regrettably isn't the suitable environment for a sensitive boy like Carroll."

Naive as he was, he had known exactly what they meant; they had all thought he was a homosexual, a queer. He had, in fact, been expelled one time after he was discovered in bed with an older boy. He was twelve and the other boy—James Something—was seventeen. Looking back after all these years, Carroll could tell now that the other boy was experienced—had probably cut a swath through all the lower forms—but he had responded to James's overtures out of a desperate need for human contact. He wanted to be held, to be cherished. They had been in bed only moments before the proctor had burst in on them in that humiliating scene, so he had never known what might have happened, but his own clear memory was of the scent of James's warm body and the spicy hair tonic the older boy affected. For one brief instant, Carroll had felt as secure as he had ever remembered being, pretending the other boy was his older brother. The desire for physical sex with another person didn't stir in him until the summer he met Elinor.

He had never understood how Elinor MacGowan had assumed complete power over him from the moment they met. She was an attractive woman, to be sure, but not beautiful, no prettier than many other women of her age. She had flaws apparent even to a smitten youth: she was willful, she was self-centered, she was vain, and—most alarming to someone as passive as he—was relentless in her pursuit of whatever she wanted at the moment, putting every atom of her being into obtaining her desire, then losing interest once she had achieved it.

Perhaps it had been as simple as the fact that she had wanted him. In the thrill of being courted, Goslin blinded himself to the motives that made her seek him out. Dazzled, he couldn't see that underneath Elinor's bravado and outward assurance in her writing talents, was a black void of insecurity, encompassing not only her fears about her writing talents, but about being alone in New York, about competing with students almost young enough to be her children, about her fears of advancing age and her husband's infidelities.

Once she was sure that he was attracted to her, she fastened onto him like a limpet on a piling, and had turned upon him the full force of her sweetness and humor and charm—for she had those traits in abundance too—concentrated like a burning glass upon an ant.

For the first time in his life, Carroll was sated with attention, found the companionship he craved, and became hers to do with as she pleased. And, like any person given total control over another human being, Elinor used her power neither wisely nor well. Carroll never noticed that the attention and affection she lavished on him were subtly twisted; in fact, had he looked more closely, he would have seen that Elinor's every word and act focused solely upon herself. Methodically, she fashioned from the boy a wheel and spokes to revolve about the hub of her own boundless ego.

Even when they had a date, Elinor always seemed utterly astonished to see him. "Why, Carroll! Come on in. I was just thinking about you, my dear." She took his hand. "I just know you can help me out on one teensy little thing. You're such a smart boy, it won't take but a moment now that you're here." Elinor would kiss him on the cheek and draw him inside the door, smiling her deprecatory smile of helpless need as she gestured toward a pile of manuscript pages.

"But Ellie," Carroll might begin. "It's nearly seven. I was hoping we'd have time for a quick supper together before I have to go back and finish my story for class tomorrow. It's not going too well, and I wanted to talk it over with you at dinner."

"You silly boy," she laughed. "You're so clever, you'll knock it together in an hour—you always do. There'll be plenty of time after dinner, and I just need a smidgen of help right now for my new chapter. Besides, I won't be able to eat a single bite until it's done."

She pouted in a fashion that brooked no resistance and pressed on. "You're so inventive with plots and boring old things like that that—it won't take you a minute to find what's gone wrong." Elinor's voice was light and teasing, but Carroll felt the old, cold feeling in his stomach. He knew that she would go on, and on, and on—for as long as it took to make him do what she wanted. He sighed. "Here. Let me take a look."

He feared, but could not contradict, Elinor's revisionism. She would repaint a given situation in whatever colors pleased her eye. In point of fact, Carroll didn't knock his pieces together in an hour. He tried often, but in vain, to explain to her that many nights he was awake until dawn, laboriously writing and reworking his stories for the next day. Elinor, he knew, not only would have done her homework, but having picked his brain and drained his energy over her novel as well, would be peacefully asleep.

Carroll had baulked once or twice, but the fury she turned on him was so consuming, that any budding resistance was feeble and short-lived.

"Well," she'd storm, "if you're going to act like that when I'm in trouble and all I've asked you to do is to read a few simple little pages, you're certainly not the friend I thought you were. Perhaps we'd better just call it quits right now, Mr. Carroll Goslin. I suppose you'd rather chase after that little blonde chit who sits in the front row with her skirt hiked up to here, rather than help me."

Carroll, horrified at the accusation, would abjectly beg her forgiveness. Elinor's endless, unjustified jealousies cowed him, her oblique thrusts and parries bewildered him and threw him off balance—what blonde was she talking about?—making him guilty over crimes he had never dreamed of committing. His terror came, too, from the fear that she would cut him loose from the only closeness he had ever known, would abandon him and force him to go home empty-handed to Mother. In the end, he felt obligated not only to help Elinor whenever she asked, at whatever personal cost, but to reassure her constantly that he was not performing the myriad unspeakable acts her imagination projected onto him.

CHAPTER SIXTEEN

"How did they ever have time for arguments and affairs?" asked Thibodeau plaintively as he rummaged through Jefferson's papers Sunday morning. "Looks like your parents spent most of their time writing letters. Your father had a violent opinion about everything, and he scribbled it down and fired it off somewhere."

"Tell me about it," said Gwendolyn, shaking her head. "Did you turn up any letters from his sister yet?"

"No. But I've got a bit more to go. I set aside some of his correspondence from Monica, but it's nothing we don't already know: their affair, Eric. She didn't discuss your mother, except to ask after the two of you once in a while. We need to find someone that your father let his hair down to."

Thibodeau was working at the picnic table, which Gwendolyn had scrubbed down and they had moved over in front of the garage. Jefferson's letters were stacked over most of the surface; the late morning air was warm, and there was no breeze to disturb them.

"If you'll clear a spot," suggested Gwendolyn, "I'll go in and make some lunch. I'll check on Eric and Patricia, and see if they'd like something too."

"I think they're in the living room watching *Casablanca*—Hanley's going to be ruined after this assignment."

"And I've contributed to the mental decay of a minor, introducing Eric to video cassettes, but there are worse fates."

"Where's Eric?"

Patricia Hanley tore her attention away from Victor McLaglen, who was sealing his doom in *The Informer*. "Why, he was here just a minute ago. We just finished *Casablanca*—maybe he went to the bathroom or up to his room."

"You're not supposed to let him out of your sight!" cried Gwendolyn, shocked at her anger.

Pat Hanley stood up at once. "I'll check upstairs."

"Eric?" Gwendolyn called anxiously as she hurried down the hall. The bathroom was off the hall to the left just before the kitchen. Eric wasn't there, nor was he in the kitchen. Then Gwendolyn saw that the cellar door in the rear of the kitchen was ajar, and she could hear noises in the basement. She let out a sigh and realized only then that she had been holding her breath. She yanked open the door and saw Eric looking up from the bottom of the stairs.

"What on earth are you doing down there? You're not supposed to wander away without letting one of us know. It's okay, he's in the basement," Gwendolyn called out to Patricia as she dashed into the kitchen.

"I just wanted to explore a bit," Eric explained contritely as

Gwendolyn came down to join him. "I came into the kitchen for something to drink, and I saw the other door and thought I'd sneak a look."

"You don't have to sneak, here, Eric. Come on, I'll show you around." The basement air was deliciously cool after the oppressive heat in the garage. "The previous owners let their teenage son live down here," she explained. "They put in paneling and flooring and made it pretty livable, but the main part had been in good shape from the beginning."

"It's huge."

"It has the same configuration as the upper floors of the house, and I figured out once that each floor has about a thousand square feet. When the place was first built, the main kitchen was down here in the back, and the food was sent upstairs in a dumbwaiter and served in the main dining room to the gentlefolk.

"The boy used this big front area for a shop—he was into motorcycles—and had his room in the back." She led Eric back down the corridor that ran from the main front room past the boiler room. Gwendolyn shook the knob on a wide door that faced the boiler room door across the hallway. It had a meshed glass window about two feet square that looked out onto the side yard and was secured by a heavy bolt inside. "That little ramp was probably put in so the kid could get his motorcycles in and out," she continued.

Gwendolyn opened a door at the end of the hallway that had been roughly framed into a Sheetrock partition.

"They knocked together a little apartment of sorts here," she said. "When I looked through the house before I bought it, I thought I might renovate the cellar and rent it out. But I never got around to it, and I don't want any other people in here anyway."

Gwendolyn fell silent, twisting her ring nervously. She had almost blurted out, "Why, it would be perfect for you, if we fixed it up a bit."

They stepped into a room about fifteen feet deep running the full width of the basement. It had been cleared and swept out, but a few broken pieces of furniture remained, a sprung sofa, once slate-blue but now gray with wear, a tattered, brown plaid armchair, and a small, three-legged table whose empty fourth corner had been jammed over the arm of the couch to prop it upright. There was a door below the kitchen that, one could see through its two narrow windows, led out into the back yard. The far right corner of the room had been partitioned off into a smaller cubicle.

Gwendolyn recovered herself and plunged on with her description. "There's a half bath over there in the corner, a sink, and toilet. The kid must have showered upstairs. When I first saw the place, there was a hot plate and a little refrigerator, so he could keep pretty much to himself. He even had his own private entrance."

"That must've been really neat," said Eric. "It must be wonderful to come and go when you want—and to work with motorcycles. I buy the cycle magazines now and then, I dream of just flying along …"

"That reminds me," Gwendolyn interrupted. "Come back out here." She pulled the door to behind them and went to the boiler room. "It's not exactly a motorcycle, but I bought a bike a while back to get some exercise but never followed through. It's been sitting in here for about five years. Do you know how to ride a bike? No? Then, if you like, we could take some time tomorrow and give you a lesson."

"I ... I don't know. I might fall off."

"You might," Gwendolyn agreed. "But if you learn to ride a bike, the next step can be a scooter or a motorcycle."

She watched his eyes go studiedly blank. The thought of getting closer to a machine than the pages of a magazine was obviously a foreign and frightening concept.

"Oh, they cost a lot, Gwendolyn. That's just a dream."

Gwendolyn didn't pursue the topic.

"What's going on down there?" Thibodeau shouted from the top of the stairs and then clattered on down to meet them. "Say, this is quite a space," he said, stepping out into the middle of the big front room. "This must be what, twenty? Twenty-five feet square? Perfect for my trains!"

"Your trains?" exclaimed Gwendolyn and Eric simultaneously. "You didn't tell me you had trains, Warren," said Gwendolyn.

"Well, 'my trains' as in 'When I win the lottery'," he laughed. "Ever since I was a kid I swore that someday I'd have a huge room with a whole setup of HO-gauge trains. The works: little bushes and trestles and empty lots and wrecked cars ... All my friends wanted to build Pacific Northwest dioramas, with snow-capped mountains and rivers and forests, while I wanted to create slums with little garbage dumps and abandoned cars and those old buildings and warehouses you see when you're pulling into the big cities."

Thibodeau went on, caught up in his fantasy. "When you take the train from Boston to New York, there's a big, run-down factory just over the Connecticut line—on your right; I *always* sit on the right. It has a sign that advertises in huge, white, peeling letters, *Wire Grilles for Prisons and Insane Asylums.* I'd kill to have a six-inch model of that ..."

They stared at him for a moment and then Gwendolyn found her voice. "I was just telling Eric that I've got a bicycle in the boiler room that he can use to learn on, if he likes."

"That's a terrific idea," said Thibodeau. "Get you out of this house a bit and into the sunshine. We could take a break tomorrow and go over to Jamaica Pond. There are paths and plenty of grassy areas to start on, so you won't get hurt if you fall off."

Eric stiffened at the words "fall off" but didn't say anything. He was used to appealing to a woman for sympathy but didn't want to look weak in front of Thibodeau.

"I'm famished," said Gwendolyn to cover Eric's silence. "Let's go up and get our lunch."

"It's a girl's name," Gwendolyn mumbled through a mouthful of sandwich. She took a swallow of coke and tried again. "It's a girl's name!"

"What are you talking about?" asked Thibodeau. "What's a girl's name?"

Gwendolyn swung her legs over the bench and began to pace up and down in front of the garage. She stopped and twirled her ring around on her finger. "My mother. When the man handed me the Christmas present, she said, 'Darling, say "Thank you" to Carol'—I'm sure it was Carol. But I didn't know any Carol then except a little red-headed girl at school. Mother couldn't have meant her."

"Keep thinking," urged Thibodeau. "It must be in there somewhere. Carroll can be a man's name, too, you know, like Evelyn or Marian, like John Wayne."

"His was Marion ..."

"Movie freak—what I'm saying is, focus on the man you saw with the present and let your mind float."

"Damn it, Warren. That's as far as I can get. Carol. Carroll. If that was the man in the photographs, why was he at the house? How would she have dared to bring him there?"

"Think about the book, Gwen. If we're right that she modeled it on a real person and herself, maybe the guy was so much younger that your mother could pass him off as just a friend. Maybe he came down for Christmas that year simply as a fellow student—a cover—or maybe that's all he was at first, and the relationship changed to an affair later on. It could be any one of a number of things. At least it gives us one name to work with."

While Gwendolyn joined Thibodeau in reading her father's letters, Eric, unbidden, stacked the plates and glasses and took them into the kitchen and then wandered out into the garage through the side door and began idly poking through the boxes.

"Finally," exclaimed Gwendolyn. "Some letters from my aunt. Here—you take this batch, and I'll do the rest." They read for a while in silence.

Eric looked around vaguely, dreaming of being on a huge, black Triumph, the wind blowing in his face making his eyes water. He could smell the leather of his new jacket and felt the pulse of the 750cc engine beneath him, the grip of his leather gauntlets on the throttle ...

He focused suddenly on a packet of blue papers on top of one of the open boxes. Airmail letters, like the ones his mother had read so often. He felt a queer shiver of recognition as he looked at the heavy, black writing—it was his mother's unmistakable, bold hand. Eric glanced at Gwendolyn and Thibodeau, but they were engrossed in their reading.

Eric scooped up the envelopes and went hurriedly out across the patio into the kitchen. His first thought was to go up to his room, where he could be alone, but after a moment's reflection, complete openness seemed to offer him the best cover. He strolled into the living room where Pat Hanley was seated at Gwendolyn's desk going over some paperwork.

"I'm sorry if I alarmed you this morning," he said as calmly as his excitement would permit. "I'm going to stay in here and read for a while."

She nodded at him and waved her hand as though to signal approval. Eric went to the window seat and bent over the letters. They were, indeed, from his mother, and were addressed to a Jefferson Davis MacGowan, at a post office box in Atlanta, Georgia. He felt a sudden reluctance to look at them but was drawn irresistibly to open one that was postmarked March 7, 1969, just days after he was born.

"Did your whole family talk in code?" Thibodeau shook his head as he puzzled over another in the growing pile of letters at his elbow.

"What do you mean? Are more of those weird letters mixed in with these?"

"No, this one's from your aunt, but she's speaking in riddles like the rest of your tribe."

"Oh?"

Thibodeau cleared his throat and began to read pompously. "'So the swans are singing lustily, and the old gander has to dance to her tune again? Must he follow everywhere the old, gray goose flaps?'"

"That sounds like dear Aunt Rachel," said Gwendolyn. "I can guess at what she meant. I remember these big rows when she would visit, because my mother would include her in all her elaborate social events, and Aunt Rachel would bitch and moan about being dragged from pillar to post, as she put it. I think she secretly liked all the hoorah, though. She didn't have any social life of her own, as far as I can tell, but she still felt she had to complain about Mother. They went to the opera once, and Rachel talked about them sounding like a bunch of 'dying swans.' I know she had a collection of uncomplimentary names for Mother—'the Old, Gray Goose' was one. Maybe if she were annoyed at my father for going along with Mother, she'd call him a gander. Anyway, it sounds like some reference to something she'd done while she was visiting here."

"You're probably right," conceded Thibodeau. "She begins by thanking him for a 'lovely—as usual—visit,' and the page is still dripping wet with sarcasm. Why visit if she hated your mother so much?"

"Spite, as far as I could tell. I heard her say once that she always thought she and my father would live together when they grew up, and she couldn't stand the idea that anyone else had her little brother. When she was here—and I know this because I was old enough to be in the middle—she would play up to whomever my father was seeing at the moment and try to help her case along. I think she would have loved to break my parents up, even though she would have hated the next woman as much if she'd succeeded."

"Here's another. 'Darling, I just got your last letter and can only say I do not understand why you continue to put up with it. It's as plain as the nose on your face what she's up to: the goose is wickeder than the gosling, and you must not let it continue! I would …'"

"What did you say? Warren! Read that last bit again!" Gwendolyn had crumpled the letter she was reading in her fist and was leaning forward across the table.

Startled, Thibodeau did as she asked. "… the goose is wickeder than the gosling …"

"That's it!" Gwendolyn cried. "That's the name! How could I have forgotten it? I heard them shouting it enough times. 'Gosling' or 'Gosslin' or something. That's the man who handed me the gift. Mother kept saying, 'Darling, say "Thank you" to Carroll, to Mr. Goslin!'"

CHAPTER SEVENTEEN

E ach day he still woke in the room where he had passed his boyhood; rose from the single bed spread with his grandmother's red-and-blue Wagon Wheel quilt, reaching for the maroon terrycloth bathrobe, a gift from Mother twenty Christmases ago, hung to dry every morning after his shower and then precisely folded and placed at the foot of the bed each night. A spacious room—though by no means as large as Mother's—it was still sparsely furnished with a dresser and leather easy chair. A double bookcase held nineteenth-century novels by the great English, French, and Russian authors and several worn handbooks on Cichlidae.

As a child, the only pets he had been permitted were fish, and when he moved back north, he set up two fifty-gallon tanks in his room, with heater, pump, lights, and all the ancillary equipment, and stocked it with an assortment of tropical fish. At first it was soothing to watch their bright patterns at night weaving about the lighted tanks, darting through the green grasses, but the play of so many colors and the eccentricity of rhythms of the different varieties made him anxious. Cichlids appealed to him, for no reason that he could articulate, so he confined himself to blue and gold specimens and discarded the others.

But now there were the letters to look forward to—not as frequent as he might like, but funny, teasing, filled with gossip about Atlanta society and unflattering remarks about Jefferson, whose philandering had increased in direct proportion to his waning powers in his financial and sexual arenas.

He had summoned the courage in his very first letter to remind Elinor again of his disappointment at the dedication in *The Ceremony of Innocence.* He'd trembled to think of her response, but he was thrilled when the next week's post brought him a fresh copy. The offending page had been conspicuously removed, and a warm inscription in her hand covered the inner front cover.

He now went out occasionally, each time looking in on Mother's room to let her know that he was doing her bidding. Her eyes bore into him as they always had, but now he had the upper hand. Out of habit, he still kept to his library job, and one day in late June saw an announcement posted for an upcoming exhibit of William Faulkner first editions and manuscripts. Elinor had spoken to him frequently of her fascination with Southern writers—Eudora Welty, Flannery O'Connor, and Faulkner particularly. She'd giggle at the knowledge that Jefferson had been born and raised (to his chagrin) in a tiny town in north central Mississippi. "Smack dab," Elinor would laugh, "in the middle of Faulkner territory." Perhaps out of some literary affinity— perhaps just to annoy Jefferson—Elinor had begun her own small Faulkner collection of signed first editions. He recalled her pride as she'd waved a copy of *Notes on a Horse Thief* before him on one visit to her home, bragging that the author had signed only 950 of them.

He bid his usual farewell to Mother one balmy afternoon when he was off duty and walked back over to the library. Even on a Thursday, there was a fair crowd gathered. There were a substantial number of personal objects along with the printed matter, including Faulkner's old Underwood—perhaps just a look-alike, but it made for a nice human touch.

A sudden movement caught his eye—an older woman was talking to someone beside a display case. Her back was toward him, but he stopped dead—the short hairs rising on the nape of his neck, his heartbeat accelerating. He *knew* that airy gesture.

Ironically, had he met her face-to-face, he might not have recognized her, one of innumerable elderly women out for an afternoon intellectual foray. But that imperious little gesture, as though she were dismissing an underling, struck his memory like a flashing blade and he cried out, "Elinor!" without thinking. Before he could begin to be embarrassed at calling out to a stranger, the woman turned, and, not missing a beat, Elinor MacGowan trilled, "Carroll Goslin? I do declare, that *is* you!"

She walked away from whoever had caught her attention at the display case, marched right up to him, and took his arm as though they were meeting in the Village for dinner after class.

"Why, imagine running into you here!" she cried gaily. "Sit down and tell me all about yourself." She pulled him over to a bench and took charge of him just as she always had.

They met as often as he could persuade her to be with him, sometimes even in her rooms at Copley Court. At those times, for her own unknowable reasons, she was coy and secretive, making a game of his having to appear at the basement door at the appointed time, then holding the door open part way, blocking it with her body until she was sure there was no one nearby in the hallway to see him enter. Each time, in exactly the same fashion, she then rushed him down to the elevator alcove and directly on up to her floor. During these maneuvers she'd giggle and refer to herself by her old code name, *Evie*. Carroll, at first nonplussed, began to see her eccentric behavior as "very Elinor"—even romantic—and threw himself into the role of secret lover.

She never offered any comprehensive explanation of her presence—how long she had actually been in town, or when exactly she'd planned on getting in touch with him. Despite her cloak-and-dagger playfulness, Elinor maintained a certain aloofness, and, despite her initial vague explanation of her presence—that she didn't want to go "west" and that he had always made Boston sound so exciting, and her oft-repeated assurance that she had *just been on the verge* of letting him know she was now living in town—he ached to know precisely *when* she had arrived, and why had she chosen this *particular* time. There was a distance between them that he was determined to close.

"This is lovely," he began by complimenting her as they sat together late one afternoon in the first week in August in her living room. "But tell me again, why did you come to Boston? I was sorry to hear that Jefferson died," he added perfunctorily, "but I thought you might decide to live with your daughter. Where is she, anyway?"

Elinor never had spoken of the girl's—he still thought of Gwendolyn as a child—exact whereabouts. Once he managed to extract, "Oh, Carroll, I've told you—Gwennie has a life of her own. Out there—" She gestured vaguely at the window in the direction of the sinking sun. "Gwennie does so love the West Coast. I've told you before"—Had she? He couldn't remember, now—"that she bought her own home and that dear little art shop where she sells photographs and prints—and frames and things. I wouldn't dream of intruding on her life. But let's talk about us. Let me look at you, Carroll!" She'd leaned toward him and smiled into his eyes with her own penetrating blue ones until he surrendered. He sipped at his tea and pushed a petit four about on his plate with a tiny silver fork.

They usually walked in the good weather or sat at a nearby café and lingered over a coffee or aperitif. They went to see *Beetlejuice*, which left them both puzzled, and Carroll splurged a substantial sum on matinee orchestra tickets for *Les Miserables* at the Schubert. It was the first time, he realized with chagrin, marveling at the show and Elinor's nearness, that he'd ever set foot inside that famous theater, and vowed it would mark just the first of many such shared excursions now that they were together again.

Just three weeks ago—a Wednesday—as they were out walking, Goslin gathered his courage and invited Elinor into his brownstone. It was not really a spur-of-the-moment decision—he'd been planning for several weeks now and had arranged for the downstairs living and dining rooms to be vacuumed, scrubbed, and aired, the drapes dry-cleaned and pulled back with their tasseled silk cords to let in the light.

It was not a far walk from Copley Court; they had occasionally strolled by it on their outings without his telling her it was his home. He was heartened that Elinor was visibly intrigued by the idea of seeing where he lived.

Not considering that Elinor would refuse his invitation, Goslin had gone to several of his favorite Charles Street shops and laid in an array of the delicacies she used to fancy—a bottle of Moët & Chandon and some raspberry-mango sorbet. Everything was waiting in the kitchen to be opened and set out. He had found and cleaned several of Mother's cut-glass vases and had them filled with brilliant sprays of flowers and foliage, heavily accented in golds, yellows, and burnt orange, remembering Elinor's predilection for yellows. If he had looked in the great gilt-framed mirror over the fireplace, Goslin would have seen himself smile: the room was alive with light and color, something he hadn't experienced since Sarah's death.

As she had in his imagination, Elinor first demurred—she never consented to *anything* right off—but then let him take her arm as they ascended the high stone steps to the entrance. Inside, he escorted her to the living room and bade her have a seat on the velvet sofa in front of the fireplace. He regretted not being able to provide a crackling fire for the perfect atmosphere, but it wouldn't be practical in mid-August, and the flue hadn't been cleaned in decades. He had made sure that the brass andirons had been polished and had purchased a prohibitively expensive bundle of small, rich logs to adorn them.

"You just relax, Evie, and I won't be a minute getting us a bite to eat."

He returned shortly, bearing a heavily laden tray and set it down on the long, low table in front of the sofa.

Goslin watched as Elinor ate with great gusto, exclaiming over the tiny sandwiches of anchovy paste, and shrimp, and scallops wrapped in bacon. They each had two flutes of cold champagne, Elinor declining a third.

"Why, Carroll, we have to walk back there and I don't want

to come in tipsy. Let me just take a look around this lovely room." Pausing by the front bay window, she exclaimed, "This is just like Gwennie's!"

"What? I thought you'd never visited …" Goslin's heart clenched. He hoped he had not caught Elinor in another one of her lies.

Elinor quickly moved around to the champagne bottle and poured them each another glass. "Oh, silly boy, I haven't—but you know those big old Victorian homes out in San Francisco. She has one and has sent me photos. I'd love one of those big windows with a lovely, soft seat looking out over the bay. She's up on a big ole hill," she says.

Mollified, Goslin raised his glass and Elinor touched it with hers, smiling her guileless smile. "What a lovely fireplace—do you use it often in the winter?"

Goslin considered their little banquet to have been a success beyond his dreams. Walking back to Copley Court, they both had been a bit tipsy; Elinor had clung to his arm and requested that he visit her in her rooms on Friday. She had something special to tell him.

He was somewhat taken aback then, when, once they were seated with tea following Elinor's little entry ritual, she looked at him expectantly and asked, "Have you kept up with your writing?" This was the first time since their meeting in the library that she'd asked. Without allowing him time to answer, she rushed on, "You'll never guess! I found that old manuscript I was working on years ago, and I brought it up here with me. I've decided, now that Jefferson is gone—I can't for the life of me understand why he made such a fuss about that book—that I'm going to finish it after all—and you can help me, just like you used to. Won't that be fun!"

Carroll felt a passing qualm at her use of "fun," but he immediately grasped at the suggestion of their working together again, of this time forming a true collaboration on a novel. He agreed, and Elinor promised to have a copy ready for him the next time they got together. In fact, uncharacteristically, she set a date right then for him to come right back to Copley Court Monday. She would meet him at their usual rendezvous at three that afternoon.

Elinor wore the same look of excitement she always wore when her work was praised in class or when she had read him a new chapter as she led him into her apartment Monday afternoon. "Sit down," she ordered, nodding at the couch and vanishing into her bedroom, returning in a moment with a cardboard box.

"I don't know where my carbon got to, but I had the original, and I had a copy made on one of those marvelous machines they have now. Here—" she thrust the carton with its Copy Quick logo into his hands. "Take this and read it as soon as you can. I can't wait to hear what you think!" She smiled and gazed at him with those clear, blue eyes, so empty of guile even when at her most manipulative.

"Of course," he hastened to assure her. "I'll read it as soon as I can, but can we just sit and talk for a bit, now?" The heady weight of the manuscript in his lap anchored Carroll. With this new bond between them, with Jefferson and Mother both out of the picture, now might be the time to approach Elinor with his plan. Surely she would prefer to live with him in his grand, private townhouse rather than here in Copley Court, which, comfortable though it might be, was after all, nothing more than a glorified old folks' home.

Elinor sat facing him, deportment-school-straight on the edge of her chair, watching him. Waiting.

Goslin scanned his closet. There was very little choice, for variety in clothing, as well as tropical fish, rendered him anxious and depressed. He kept his garments hung neatly and in order, several each of slacks, jackets, shirts, and dark ties on a little carousel, beside the long black coat.

Yesterday he had purchased several new items, and he now picked out the black jogging outfit—a hooded sweatshirt and elastic-bottomed pants with roomy pockets in both garments— and the pair of thick-soled running shoes and put them on the bed. He set the new tan canvas duffel bag beside them and packed it with two pairs each of T-shirts, underwear, and socks.

He pulled on the sweat suit and inspected himself in the full-length mirror on the closet door before returning to his packing. He added a shaving kit from his dresser drawer and then he picked out several items from a box on the floor next to the dresser, examining each carefully before putting it into the duffel bag: two pairs of handcuffs and a single key that fit them both, a Swiss army knife, a roll of duct tape, a small pair of binoculars, a glass cutter, rubber disc and putty, and, finally, the knife and gun. He made sure he had money in the Velcro-flapped back pocket of the sweat suit pants, checked that he had the handcuff key secured, then turned on the aquarium lights and shook extra food into the fish tank. He tapped the glass lightly in a gesture of farewell.

Eric stumbled out the front door with the packet of airmail letters. He had only read the one; he didn't want to know more. His eyes were red, and his breath was catching in unvoiced sobs. He walked past Patricia, still engrossed in her paperwork, then out the front door and the long way around the house, to the patio, so that he came unnoticed to the side door of the garage.

He was consumed with loss and anger—loss of a father now doubly dead, and anger at all these people who had obviously known the truth all along, but who hadn't seen fit to tell a poor, crippled half-wit the truth.

Eric slipped into the garage and set the letters back where he had found them. He didn't know whether they were in the same order, or whether they had been in any order at all. He didn't care. He took several deep breaths to compose himself, then strode out to the picnic table, noticing as he emerged into the bright light that Gwendolyn was alone at the table stacking papers. Thibodeau and his car were gone.

"Hi! Come on over and sit with—what's wrong?" Gwendolyn's cheerful tone changed to one of concern when she saw the boy's face.

"I'm … just thinking about Mother," Eric answered truthfully. He wiped his eyes with the back of his wrist and sat down opposite Gwendolyn.

"I finally remembered the name of the man who may be the killer," said Gwendolyn. "Warren has gone downtown to start the process of tracking him down. Won't it be a tremendous relief to know he's been put away, and to have this all over?"

"Will it be over then? I still don't know what will happen to me. Was Mr. Thibodeau able to reach my aunt?"

Gwendolyn was puzzled by the coldness and reserve in Eric's voice, which hadn't been there before. Just when he'd been opening up a bit, too. "I don't know if he has or not. We'll ask him when he comes back. Will you help me get these papers into the house, please? I thought we might get out for a while. I want to pick up a few groceries, and I need to gas up the car."

Silently, he helped her put the letters into a box and followed her inside to the living room.

"Patricia," said Gwendolyn. "I'm going out to the grocery store. I want to stock up now, ahead of the Labor Day crush. Can I pick up anything for you while I'm gone?"

Officer Hanley shuffled her notes together and pushed back from the desk. "Remember, you don't go anywhere without me. My job is to guard you, not the house, so where you go, I go. Wouldn't mind getting out myself, anyway."

"Okay," Gwendolyn agreed. "Your car is parked behind mine. If you'll move it over in front of the picnic table, I'll back mine out of the garage. Do you need to get anything, Eric?"

"I'd like to take a wash and get my jacket," he said, starting upstairs. Thibodeau had brought over their suitcases from the hotel, so Eric now had his own belongings—although she had been amused to notice him wearing her old pajamas one morning. He was a long time returning, and when he came out to the car, it was obvious he had been crying.

"I'll make one last check of the doors," said Gwendolyn. She returned a few minutes later, nodding her head in approval. "All set," she said as she got into the driver's seat. "Warren has a spare key in case he gets back before we do."

Pat Hanley sat up front with Gwendolyn, while Eric huddled silently in the back. The heat had broken a bit, and there was a cool breeze blowing as Gwendolyn drove down the Jamaicaway and out Brookline Avenue toward Fenway Park.

"We're making good time, today, folks," said Gwendolyn, trying to make conversation. "I usually hit ballgame traffic no matter when I drive out this way." She pulled into the parking lot of a big Star Market and found a space near the entrance. "Would you all like fried chicken tonight? It's one of the few things I can cook."

"Sure. I love fried chicken," said Patricia. "I usually have to eat it on the run out of a bucket. I'll make a salad, if you like."

"Thanks," said Gwendolyn, grateful for the conversation as much as the offer. She turned to the silent Eric, who simply shrugged his shoulders. "Well, come along, then. If you see anything you'd like, just put it in the cart. Pick yourself out a treat or two."

They filed into the store, Eric and Patricia trailing after Gwendolyn as she picked up milk, juice, salad fixings, Cokes, fresh chicken, and frozen dinners. Eric became more animated as he explored the supermarket. An average Star Market, it was gigantic by comparison with Eric's village shop, and Gwendolyn noticed with amusement his additions of chocolate bars, chips, and cookies.

They had dinner prepared and on the table by the time Thibodeau returned. Before he could sit down, Gwendolyn demanded, "So, what's happened—did you find a Carroll Goslin?"

"Wish I could say we had. It doesn't look to be that easy. I went through the DMV first, but there's no car registered to him, and no current license issued to a Goslin who would be anywhere near his age or description, and no Carroll or C. Goslin anywhere in the area. But if we assume that the place he took Eric was his own home, then it's got to be somewhere within walking distance of the Common. Eric may have wandered quite a bit before he got to the bus station, but he didn't come in from Brookline or Chelsea or Cambridge. And that North Shore drive on Thursday had to have been a red herring, because he certainly couldn't have walked back from there. The guy could be living under an assumed name, or maybe you remembered the wrong name, or Carroll Goslin was the right name but the wrong man."

"I'm sure it's the name," insisted Gwendolyn. "Bits of things are coming back to me, little fragments of their arguments. I remember my father making innuendos about 'a Nancy boy who would call himself Carroll.' I think there's a lot of that kind of thing I've blocked out of my mind."

"The guy seems certifiable so far," commented Patricia. "So maybe he's the man you remember, but he kept himself in hiding all these years."

"But that doesn't make any sense either, Pat—may I call you Pat? Mother must have known he was living in Boston, because of the postmarks on the letters. Maybe he communicated his address to her in one of their code things—like banks and credit companies are always asking for your mother's maiden name."

"That's a thought," said Thibodeau. "Do you know anything about this guy's family?"

171

"No," replied Gwendolyn, "or if I did, it certainly didn't register. I was just a kid, and remembering any names of people I met was quite a feat for me, much less wondering about their mother's names. I only met him that once, that I recall, though of course he may have been around in the background, like my father's lady friends—and I certainly never asked about them. I don't even know what Goslin did. Now if Mother had only said, 'Darling, say "Thank you" to Carroll Goslin, shipwright, whose mother, née Fiona Hogmanay, is the famous Vedic scholar,' and if I had only filed that away in my eidetic memory ... But I'm afraid I've shot my bolt with Carroll Goslin."

"'... famous Vedic scholar who lives with her son at Hogmanay's End on St. Botolph Street, Boston,' would have been even better, Gwen," laughed Thibodeau, "but we'll have to go with what we've got."

Pat Hanley and Gwendolyn began to elaborate, piling on more details she should have remembered, '... with the mole on her left knee,' '... whose telephone number is ...' All three were laughing uproariously when Gwendolyn stopped short, noticing that Eric had not joined in.

CHAPTER EIGHTEEN

With his thick hair and unlined face, Carroll Goslin looked younger than his years as he walked west on Newbury Street toward his car. In his running suit, he could easily have been taken for a middle-aged businessman heading out to the squash courts.

He quickly discovered it was much too hot for the jacket, so he took it off and tied the sleeves around his waist. His arms, unexposed to the sun for years, were dead white—smooth-skinned and hairless. What once might have become an athletic body was, through a lifetime of disuse, unformed and flaccid, its physical potential long ago dissipated.

Goslin felt exposed outdoors without his hat and coat, but after a few blocks discovered that the light breeze in his hair and the loose, comfortable clothing was rather pleasant. His blood began to pump, and he felt an unaccustomed surge of energy— then realized that it derived from his anticipation of the mission at hand.

He enjoyed the feel of the soft cotton brushing his skin, and the lightness of his new sneakers—"jogging shoes," the salesman

173

had called them—added spring to his long stride. He felt a simple animal pleasure in the heat of the sun on his face.

His car was still parked in a space near the Massachusetts Avenue end of Newbury Street—three tickets were jammed under the windshield wiper, but nothing else had been disturbed. Goslin set the duffel bag on the passenger seat and started the engine. For a moment, he had the desire to drive aimlessly, enjoying the freedom of movement and the breeze blowing through the open window. He thought of crossing the MIT bridge and passing an hour or two by the Basin, watching the flotilla of Sunday sailors skipper their small craft in an ever-changing kaleidoscope of white triangles. But duty was pressing; it wouldn't do to risk exposure by driving around any more than necessary today—he couldn't risk being stopped for some minor traffic violation and being caught without a valid driver's license.

Goslin's had expired several years ago, and, while he still carried the old one in his wallet, he had never renewed it. He hated all kinds of bureaucracy and especially hated having to appear in official places where people could observe and judge—and now photograph—him. Not having a license hadn't made a great deal of difference, anyway. He had very few places to go and could take the T or walk to most of them. As long as Mother remained well, she had driven to her favorite market in Chestnut Hill with Goslin in the passenger seat. After she became ill, Goslin had bought a little two-wheeled shopping cart and walked the few blocks to the various specialty shops on nearby Charles Street.

He kept to his plan and dutifully turned south. As he passed Fenway Park, heading for the Jamaicaway, he was struck by the numbers of people walking, jogging, and biking around Jamaica Pond, and instead of turning up Pond Street toward Centre as he had planned, he circled the little lake until he found a grassy apron at one end where other cars were parked. He stowed his duffel bag in the trunk and set off on foot, another jogger blending into the crowd.

It was just after five thirty by his watch. Goslin took a few steps toward the stoplight at Pond Street and the Jamaicaway, then, his finger on the stop button, he wavered, turned, and took a few halting steps back toward the drinking fountain by the boathouse. His earlier confidence evaporating, he began to hyperventilate, panicking in what was now a terrifying open space, shrinking from the tide of strangers flooding about him. He felt their eyes all turned on him; curious, questioning, probing … He made his way to a nearby bench and sank down, drenched with sweat.

Mother materialized in his mind's eye, her thin lips set like a razor slash, shaking her head, his pusillanimity too disgraceful for words. Her anger overrode his panic; Goslin pulled himself together and set off along the blacktop path around the pond. The physical act of walking calmed him. He tried to concentrate on the lapping water, the reflections of the willows, and the gray oblong of the Prudential building visible all the way downtown. The pad of his sneakers on the macadam, the regular strides and rhythmical swinging of his arms all served to center him, to focus him on Gwendolyn and what he had to do.

The boy was with her now, at least he suspected as much after the coverage of them both on television, and the police would be watching, perhaps even have someone on the premises. He would have to reach the house, then insinuate himself inside in such a way that he'd have all the time he needed. There would not be another chance. Goslin completed one circuit of the pond and now, breathing deeply and evenly, started another.

"Are you feeling all right, Eric? Do you have a headache or something?"

Gwendolyn frowned. Something was wrong with the boy, and she was sure it was more than a reaction to Monica's death.

"I'm all right, just rather tired. My leg aches, and I would like to go upstairs and lie down." He paused, as though waiting for her to disagree with him, ready to argue back.

"Go on, then. We'll be in the living room if you need anything."

He turned away and started to mount the stairs.

"Eric?"

Eric turned but didn't speak.

"Are you sure nothing's wrong? There's not something you'd like to talk about?"

He shook his head and turned away, pulling himself up the stairs by the banister rail like an elderly little man.

Gwendolyn grasped the newel post, yanking the unyielding oak as she watched the boy disappear around the corner at the top of the stairs, then she turned and joined Patricia and Warren in the living room.

"Warren, did Eric say anything to you this afternoon? There's something going on, but I can't pry a word out of him."

"No, nothing earthshaking. I didn't talk to him after we had lunch. He did take me aside after supper and ask if I had gotten in touch with his aunt. I told him that we found out from a neighbor that she's on vacation—a walking tour someplace unreachable north of London—and she won't be back for ten days. I hope it's not anything serious, Gwen, because you're going to have your little guest for a while longer."

"Terrific. And I don't even know if I've done anything to upset him. I'm going to make some coffee. Would either of you like something? I'm too jittery to sit still."

"I'd like some tea," said Patricia. "I'll come out and keep you company."

"Nothing for me," said Thibodeau, picking up his jacket. "I've got to be going. I'm bushed, and I've got to get an early start tomorrow. I don't like it that we don't have anything on Goslin yet. Don't go out tonight. It's been quiet the last two days, but that doesn't mean he isn't around."

Gwendolyn walked him to the front door. "Don't worry. Patricia is keeping right on Eric, and I've got my automatic in the drawer next to the bed …"

"Be careful, Gwen—it's one thing to nail a paper target at the range, and something else to shoot a human being. A firefight is a whole different ball of wax. If anything should happen—and I'm not saying it will—it's better to lie low or call 911. Leave the rest to Pat Hanley—she's the professional; that's why she's here. I'll call you tomorrow and touch base or drop by in the afternoon. Maybe we can draw Eric out a bit with that bike. If you're looking for something to do, you might take it out and pump up the tires."

"That's not a bad idea. I need to go into my shop in the morning. Margaret and Vince have been holding down the fort for the last week, but I need to get some tax material. The sales tax form was due on the 20th, and here it is the 28th—I'll pay a penalty on that. But why am I babbling about the shop? You go on home and get some rest. We'll be fine."

⁜ ⁜ ⁜

Dusk was gathering as Goslin finished his third circuit around the pond, and he noticed suddenly that most of the cars were gone, leaving his Volvo isolated and conspicuous. He checked the trunk, saw that his duffel bag was intact, then drove the car around the pond and found an out-of-the-way spot on a side street.

Goslin pushed open the door to the Galway House, a combination bar-grill on the main street of Jamaica Plain. Three televisions were blaring, and after a perfunctory glance or two from a few regulars, no one paid any attention to the newcomer. Following his ignominious return to Boston, it had become increasingly difficult for Goslin to be out among people. He never went to the movies, rarely entered restaurants or any public place if he could avoid it, but his outing in the park this afternoon had emboldened him, and he realized, too, that he must have something to eat.

He ordered vegetable soup and a corned beef sandwich and ate facing one of the huge screens surrounded by a knot of rapt fans urging on the losing Sox with shouts and gestures. For once, Goslin found a crowd of people comforting. Everyone was so obviously wrapped up in the game that he didn't feel out of place. He ordered a draught beer and nursed it until night had fallen.

"I looked in on Eric to say good night," said Gwendolyn, returning to the living room, "but he's asleep—at least the lights are out." She sat down on the couch with Patricia. "I never realized until this past week how few comfortable pieces of furniture I have."

"Don't apologize. This is a hell of a lot more comfortable than most of the stakeout work I do. And you've been very generous with refreshments. That chicken was a real treat. I don't do much cooking on my own."

"Neither do I. One day I found I was all grown up and living by myself and had no idea how to cook a meal. Steak I figured out pretty quickly, and I remembered how our maid back in Atlanta would shake chicken pieces in a brown paper bag with salt and pepper and then arrange them all in a skillet of hot Crisco. And of course, there are always frozen dinners. Tell me," she asked, "do you do much of this kind of protection work? It must be boring."

"With luck it is. Usually, I've been assigned to protect someone who's actually been threatened. This case is unusual, with two other murders, but no specific threat against you."

"I'll be a lot happier when they've caught the guy, I can tell you," said Gwendolyn. "By the way, I was just telling Warren that I want to stop by my shop tomorrow morning to get some papers. I suppose I could have them cabbed over, but I'd like to go myself. I haven't been in, in over a week now. Would that be all right with you?"

"You're the boss. But we'll all have to go. Can't leave one person here unattended."

"That makes sense. Eric will just have to come along, sulking or not." Gwendolyn got up and walked around the room pausing to kneel on the window seat and peer out the bay windows. A patrol car was cruising past the end of the driveway, under the street lamp, then on into the gloom.

✢   ✢   ✢

Carroll Goslin made his way up the street that ran along the back of Beech Hill. He passed one or two people, but no one gave him a second glance. Before leaving the restaurant, he had put on the black jacket. With the tan bag slung over his shoulder, he strolled along casually, looking about him. At the top of the hill he turned down the street where he had parked two nights before.

This time, instead of crossing the driveway, Goslin hugged the shadows of the tree trunks and worked his way toward the garage. He froze as headlights swept through the columns of the trunks. As the car passed under the streetlight, he saw that it was a police cruiser.

Inching his way to the side of the garage, he flattened himself against the wall and peered into the side window. There was a small station wagon parked on the side nearest him. There was another car parked outside the garage, confirming his suspicion that someone else was in the house.

Goslin continued on around the back of the garage and settled behind one of the broad trunks to observe the kitchen window. He felt inside the bag for the binoculars and rested against the smooth bark to steady himself as he focused.

Two women carrying cups came into the room. The taller had short, dark hair. She took the cup from the younger, redheaded woman, and turned toward him, looking down. Behind them he could see the bottoms of glass-fronted cabinets filled with dishes and glassware, and off to the left, the shiny white enamel of a refrigerator. He couldn't see their hands now, but assumed by their positions as they faced him that they were standing together at the kitchen sink, cleaning up for the evening. The taller, dark-haired one had to be MacGowan.

He felt he was right there beside them.

Off to the right, he could glimpse an open door, probably entering into a hallway leading back into the house. Beyond the refrigerator there was a closed door. The boy was nowhere in sight.

The house loomed huge and dark against the night sky, the mansard roof illuminated faintly by the city lights to the northeast. The place looked contemporary, compared with his own brownstone. It obviously contained many rooms and probably had more than one stairwell. If his own home was any example, the floorboards would creak here and there, but once the bedroom doors were shut, very little outside noise could be heard. Back in the days when Mother's bridge guests still visited, they could knock or ring for quite some time before they were noticed.

Goslin moved on, keeping in the shadow of the trees until he was past the field of view of the kitchen window. Then he hunched over, shielding the tan bag with his body, and scuttled up against the side of the house. By keeping low and crouching behind the border of box hedges, he was invisible unless someone pinned him in a flashlight beam or opened a window and looked directly down. In the latter case, the sound of a screen or window being raised would give him enough warning to escape.

As he had anticipated, the cellar door was locked, but there were windows all around the foundation opening into the basement. The nearest house on this side was at least fifty feet away, and his movements were screened not only by the boxwood, but by another tall hedge running along the property line. Its windows were dark. The residents were either out for the evening or, if he were very lucky, away for a long Labor Day holiday.

Goslin tried the wide wooden door as he passed down the side of the house, and on a sudden impulse stowed his bag in the shallow stairwell that led down to the doorway. It was easier to make his way along the perimeter of the building with his hands free. He came upon the front door just after he rounded the corner to the front of the house.

He sat back against the side of the front steps, shielded by the shrubbery, and collected his thoughts. He knew that in this kind of Victorian house it was unlikely that the front door would lead directly into a room. There would be a foyer or hallway, perhaps the front stairs. The hallway that he saw leading from the kitchen probably cut straight through the house to the front door. He would have to make sure, but if he were correct, then the side of the house along which he had just walked would offer the greatest protection.

The ground was slightly damp, and the evening air was cooling. The clipped boxwood branches brushed his cheek, and he started as something crawled across his bare hand. Goslin pushed himself upright and crept forward across the doorstep and into the bushes beyond. Bright light shone out of the open bay window, and he could hear voices and music, a radio or television program of some kind. Fascinated, he moved forward, dropping to his hands and knees until he had crawled directly under the overhang of the bay windows. He leaned his back against the wall and drew his knees up to his chest. His heart was pounding with excitement, and all trace of tiredness and panic had vanished.

He was home, inside the Keep—the coat closet off the living room—curled into a tight, motionless ball listening to Mother and her friends. The whirr of shuffled cards, the dainty chink of china cups against saucers, the laughter and the women's catty gossip excited him beyond measure. The smell of their mixed perfumes and cosmetics permeating the coats and scarves surrounding him in the darkness was as heady and voluptuous as the hard steel of the gun and the bowie knife deep in the darkness of the upstairs linen closet.

They were his only possessions of Father's, discovered late one afternoon while he was playing in the darkened linen closet; a loaded, blue-black pistol redolent of oil and violence, and a huge bowie knife with a Damascus steel blade patterned like reptile skin. These artifacts his father had, for reasons of his own, wrapped in soft flannel cloths and hidden in a wooden box at the very back of the bottom shelf. Carroll knew instinctively that to remove them would cause them to be found and taken from him. He rewrapped them and left them exactly where Father had secreted them, incorporating them from time to time into his own secret games, stealing to them in the darkness as to illicit lovers, and in handling them experienced the same surge of pleasure and excitement as he did when he touched himself.

Ensconced in the Keep, his excitement arose not so much from the content of the women's conversation, but from the fact that he was a secret listener and had gained the sanctuary of the closet through his own stealth and cunning. Over time, Carroll had made rather an elaborate game of the Keep—a game with specific rules. He must enter in full view of the women, and must leave before their bridge game broke up, giving them two chances to capture him. He had regretted that this was not as difficult a task as it might seem, since once they were engrossed in their game and gossip, Carroll was rendered invisible by some sort of female sorcery of male exclusion.

Perfect little gentleman that he was, Carroll would offer without prompting to hang their coats, giving him a chance to hug the still-warm furs and cloaks to his body while he entered the closet with them. Later, when the rattle of silver and china indicated that they were preparing to leave, Carroll would inch the closet door open and, standing upright, sidestep out swiftly, as though he were just entering the room. He had a second chance, then, to gather the coats and help the women on with them, mixing the smells of the garments with the odors of their warm, living flesh.

Goslin closed his eyes now and drew a deep breath, startled, so deep had he been in his reverie, to smell not perfume but buttered popcorn on the heavy evening air.

The Horse's Mouth credits rolled. Gwendolyn stood up and stretched, then fished for the VCR controls and punched the rewind button. "It's nearly eleven, Pat. I'm going to get my ice water and go up to bed. I'm worn out."

"Me too. You go ahead. I'll call the station and then come on up. I want to check the car and make sure the garage is locked. What time do you want to leave in the morning?"

"Well ..." Gwendolyn yawned. "I'd like to get a fairly early start. If we could have breakfast by eight or eight thirty and get off around nine, then I can be back here as soon as possible in case Warren calls or needs me for something. Oh," she turned at the doorway. "Don't let me forget to get my old bike out of the cellar and throw it in the back of the car. I want to get the tires filled. 'night."

Patricia Hanley made sure the front door was locked, then walked down the hall and out the back to the garage. She shook the double doors and checked the side door, shining the powerful beam around the garage and through the trees. She came in the back door and latched it behind her, then walked through the downstairs, shutting and latching the ground-floor windows. Glancing at her watch, she saw that it was twenty-five minutes after eleven. Hanley dialed the station, reporting that all was well on Beech Hill.

CHAPTER NINETEEN

Gwendolyn, clad in her light cotton pajamas, stood in the bay window of her bedroom looking out into the night. The moon was rising, the night sky clearing. She could just glimpse the stars through the dark tracery of the leaves above. All the windows on the top floor were open wide. Gwendolyn generally preferred warmth, liked to feel it as a palpable thing caressing her skin, and had never considered air-conditioning, preferring, even on the muggiest nights, to use only electric fans, but tonight she found the atmosphere oppressive.

Tired, but not sleepy, Gwendolyn knew from experience that it would be useless to lie down just yet, so she picked up a copy of Elizabeth Taylor's *Mrs. Palfrey at the Claremont* that she had bought the week her mother was killed. She laughed to herself, recalling a customer at the shop who had seen the book on the counter and had exclaimed, "Why, I didn't know that Liz wrote books, too!"

It was strange, thought Gwendolyn, letting her mind wander a moment from Mrs. Palfrey, that it had taken two violent deaths for her to find that she rather enjoyed having another human presence in the house. With a pang of regret, she wished that it had been possible to welcome Elinor into her home, but she could see even more clearly that it would never have worked. Too bad she couldn't have been more like the dignified—albeit fictional—Mrs. Palfrey; calm, unpursued by inner demons. Gwendolyn still felt she had no comprehension of what had driven her parent, but she felt a rush of compassion that she hoped was the forerunner of forgiveness.

And Eric? What was her duty—if any—to the boy? She turned restlessly, not wanting to think about him, but knowing that at some point she would have to confront the problem. He would soon legally be an adult, but as far as she could ascertain, he had no real education, training, or skills. What kind of future would he face alone back in England? Had Monica even owned the house they lived in?

She stood up and dropped the book on the chair. It was no use reading, either; she couldn't concentrate tonight. She kept thinking of the boy as "Eric" and resisted letting "brother" creep into her thoughts.

Eric lay in the darkness, his mind seething with painful and humiliating images. His sense of loss and betrayal was so acute as to be a physical pain. His chest constricted, and he gasped for breath. He raged against the woman who had lied to him his whole life, then was overwhelmed with guilt that he should feel such anger when she was even now lying cold on a slab.

He wished he had never discovered that his father was not the brave, young soldier he had been led to believe, then acknowledged that, if not for his mother's murder, he would have forever lived a lie. Who *was* he, then? He had allowed himself to become the clinging invalid his mother wanted. If he were honest with himself, he would have to admit that he'd made no effort to become healthy or to fight for what he wanted. And just what would *that* be? Whose fault was it that he had no inner reserves to fall back on now? Here he was, nearly grown, and he felt as bereft and defenseless as an abandoned child.

Was Gwendolyn part of this deception? All afternoon he had been distant and rude to her, but had she actually known about him? As usual, he hadn't bothered to ask but had sulked like a child instead of confronting the problem directly. With an outsider's eyes he saw himself yesterday morning, whining for hot tea like some pathetic Oliver Twist begging for seconds, instead of requesting, "May I have some *hot* tea?" like an adult. He thrashed about until the sheets were tangled, judging himself more harshly now than he had been lenient with himself before.

Patricia Hanley set her Smith & Wesson .38 on the bedside table and read three chapters of *The Fatal Shore* before placing it neatly beside the gun and falling at once into a deep, untroubled sleep.

Carroll Goslin, his back against the shadowed side wall, sat watching the silver moonlight dappling the beech trunks. The police cruiser drove by again, and Goslin estimated that at least a half hour had elapsed since its last round. There would be no problems as long as he remained calm.

When the light on the second floor went out, Goslin moved back among the trees, looking up at the house. One light shone faintly on the third floor, but even as he watched, it winked out. Taking his time, Goslin continued his circuit of the house. He walked past the now-darkened bay window, around the front left corner and along the driveway, following his route of Friday night. His stomach gave a queer lurch as he stepped onto the patio where Monica had been sitting. The flagstones gleamed in the moonlight which shown full upon them, and to Goslin's eyes, they seemed to shimmer and float in the blackness of the yard like steel lily pads on a lake of tar. He studied the upstairs windows for several minutes before venturing to cross the dangerous open space to gain the shelter of the box hedge on the far side of the kitchen door.

He retrieved his duffel bag from the stairwell and removed several items, including a suction disc, glass cutter, penlight, and filters. Since both cellar doors were locked, it would be necessary to go in through one of the windows. Guessing that the back door, closer to the garage and patio, was most often used for casual comings and goings, he decided to tackle a window nearer the front of the house. He examined the windows from the wide side door up to the front corner. They were, as he had anticipated, all locked, so he moved on to the side windows. He'd once seen a pair of glaziers on Charles Street removing a large shop window with suction discs and had tucked that knowledge away in his mind.

He chose the window nearest the front corner of the house, well hidden by the shrubbery. Goslin conceded to himself that he could probably get away with just breaking it but, like the Keep—no, even more than the Keep—this final Game must be played correctly; the MacGowan stronghold would be breached according to strict Game protocol.

Goslin rubbed a bit of saliva into the cup of the disc and pressed it against a pane of glass. He screwed a red filter onto the end of the penlight, switched it on, and put the light in his mouth, training the beam on the window. He ran the glass cutter around the edge of the pane, and when he gave it a sharp tap, the glass broke loose. Maneuvering the suction disc, he angled the pane out intact and set it gently on the soft earth. He reached in through the opening and felt around for the window latch. It was then a simple matter to open the window and climb down into the basement, pulling the duffel bag and the suction cup with the attached square of glass in after him. His pulse was pounding, but he observed himself with calm detachment.

Finding that he was in a large, open room with no stored objects or furniture to give him cover, he moved quickly along the wall leading toward the back of the house. As he passed, he noticed a latch on a wide wooden door and found that it opened into the boiler room. He removed the red filter from the penlight and played the beam around the room, picking out the oil burner and tanks, washer, and dryer. Against one wall was the bicycle he had heard the MacGowan woman mention earlier in the evening as he sat under the window. Someone would be coming down to get it in the morning.

Replacing the filter, Goslin picked his way down the hallway, past the stairway, and on to the end of the hall. He listened a moment at the door before slowly turning the handle. He entered and closed the door behind him, appraising the space. A delicious sense of security enveloped him, like an animal returning to its familiar lair. Some instinct told him that he had nothing to fear in this room; whatever danger he might face later on, he had found a safe haven for tonight. He fastened the hook and eye on the inside of the door and looked about him. Opening the bathroom door, he realized how thirsty he was. He eased the faucet open and drank cool water from the cup of his hand.

Earlier, he had noticed the bolt on the back door and now, refreshed, set to work with the screwdriver blade of the new jackknife. He removed all the screws, the bolt and plate, then enlarged the screw holes with the knife's auger blade. When he replaced the plate, he was able to push the screws in like tacks. He gingerly tested it, finding, as he had intended, that the bolt could be worked horizontally without revealing that it had been weakened, while if he had to get in from outside, the screws would pull out easily.

Goslin set the duffel on the bed, removing the gun and sliding the bowie knife from its thick leather sheath. He played the flashlight beam repeatedly over the rippling patterns before replacing the blade and slipping the sheath inside his pants leg, attaching it to his waistband on its pivoting metal clip. The weight dragged on the light cloth but held.

His thirst slaked, he noticed now that his stomach was gnawing with hunger. Goslin smiled. How many times had Mother sent him to bed without supper, and how many times had he won that Game, creeping past her door late at night to feast in the pantry. Like the Keep, this Game was also to be played by strict rules. When Carroll was small, he had been content to sneak down from his room and steal some cookies or a scoop of peanut butter and scurry back to his room. As he grew older, he imposed harsher restrictions upon himself. He must not merely snatch food from the refrigerator or gulp from cartons, but eat off a plate and drink from a glass. Later, the Game required that he have a cooked meal, eaten from a plate at the table, with a napkin and cutlery. In the end, he was able to take as long as he needed to cook and eat a leisurely supper without ever waking Mother.

At that point the Game palled. Carroll had become too large to be physically frightened of her, and on her part, Mother no longer punished him in an unsophisticated physical fashion, having herself progressed in what he assumed was her own version of the Game. Tonight's work had rekindled the thrill of desire and love of danger that had been his only companions long ago. Yes, he was hungry, and he knew from his earlier observations through the binoculars that he must be almost directly beneath the kitchen. Goslin stowed his loose gear in the bag and set it at the end of the couch. Taking only the filtered penlight, he closed the door to the room behind him, and set off upstairs for dinner.

The hum of the old refrigerator covered Goslin's entry into the kitchen. He paused, sniffing; the room was still redolent of fried chicken and popcorn. A small night-light above the sink illuminated the area. A good-size kitchen, it was big enough for a three-by-eight-foot butcher-block table in the center, yet still afforded plenty of space to maneuver. Double windows over the sink looked out directly into the backyard and, to the left, onto a corner of the patio. A wall of blackness bordered the back—the massive beech trunks.

Carroll sensed the sleepers upstairs, just as he used to feel Mother's shallow breath pulsing deep within his own chest. Tonight the sensation was tripled, rendered exquisitely acute by three separate entities breathing in counterpoint, helpless, unaware of his presence in the house.

Putting aside his hunger, he edged noiselessly down the hallway, a thick, patterned runner muting any creaking floorboards. From long practice he moved fluidly, the leather sheath pressed hard against his thigh, his new sneakers sinking into the thick pile. Mother always insisted that he wear only leather dress shoes but had been forced from time to time to buy him athletic shoes for his gym classes. Carroll loved those sneakers, the thin canvas snug around his ankles, the thick soles alive to his every step. Each time they returned from the shoe store after buying a new pair, he would run up to his room clutching the parcel, and, after making sure Mother hadn't followed him, he would bury his face in the open box, nuzzling the rough new fabric and inhaling the mixed odors of rubber and canvas.

A floorboard creaked slightly as Carroll reached the foot of the stairs, and he paused, alert; reminded himself that if the sleepers' doors were shut, they would have heard nothing. Take time. No need to rush. Hearing no response, he moved on into the living room. There was the bay window under which he had eavesdropped earlier; there was the television set he had heard playing. Carroll sat down on the couch and stared at the blank screen, imagining the pleasure of watching a film while the others slept on unawares. There was the popcorn bowl on the end table, still partially full. He took a handful, savoring the salty grains on his tongue and stretching his legs out full length.

But this wasn't the Game, he admonished himself. There was no danger in sitting here comfortably. To prove his worth he would have to do much, much more. He needed to earn his meal to give it savor. He returned to the stairway and eased his weight slowly onto the first step. Like his own home, this old Victorian was solidly built—the stairs firm, the balusters massive as their parent oaks. As he made his way up to the second-floor landing, there were tiny creaks, but no sound louder than an old building's usual night noises. Carroll smiled.

He pictured the fearful occupants primed for the smash of glass, the cry of the maniac, and the pounding of feet on the stairs. The police, too—what did they expect to see on their nightly rounds? A monster, wild-eyed and haggard, holding a blazing torch aloft as he pounded on the door? No, he was here as a guest. An occupant, if the truth be told. It was obvious to him that he had earned the right to be here. In a way that he could never make any of them understand, Carroll knew this *was* his home.

He hesitated on the second-floor landing, deciding whether to go directly to the top floor first or to start right here. A light, muffled snore issued from the first door off the landing. It was open a crack, and he pushed it gently with the tips of his fingers. The heavy oak yielded, swinging open smoothly on its hinges another few inches. He listened long enough to determine that the sleeper hadn't wakened, then pushed again, paused, and stepped into the room.

The shades had not been drawn, and the risen moon offered enough light for him to make out a motionless form. Its breathing was deep, but lighter than a man's. Goslin detected the faintest scent of face powder in the air. This would either be Gwendolyn or the officer—the owner of that station wagon in the garage—who had been sent to the house to protect the others.

Carroll withdrew, pulling the door closed to its original position. The next door was closed and did not yield to touch. Flattening himself against the panels, he wrapped his hand around the knob and turned it in tiny increments until the latch eased out of the lock strike. Like the first door, the second then swung open soundlessly. Carroll stopped, holding his breath. There was a dim light. Was the person awake? Reading? He could have sworn that he had felt them all sleeping.

But there was no movement or alarm. In the stillness he could hear the very faintest sound of breathing. He arced the door open, braced against his long forearm, keeping his body well behind the door. The boy. A small lamp on a bureau by the bed illuminated him clearly. He was deeply asleep, lying on one side, one arm crooked over his eyes, his knees drawn up in a near fetal position. As Carroll observed, the boy groaned and shifted over onto his back, his arm still covering his face. Carroll stared at his vulnerable form a long time before withdrawing.

He next felt his way up the stairs to the third-floor landing under a double brass fixture with frosted globes that bathed the polished hardwood of the floor and wainscoting in a warm, amber light. Four doors opening off this landing and a corridor leading back to yet another door at the far end. Gambling that the door nearest him opened onto the back stairwell, Carroll tried it and saw he was correct. He left it ajar, deciding not to risk the front stairs on his way down.

One after another, he checked the rooms grouped around the landing, determining that they were not occupied. Back stairs, a small kitchen, a large bathroom with another night-light burning, an office or storage room, and then the hallway. There was no carpeting on the top floor, and the boards had more give under his feet. Carroll willed himself to slow down, padding along the right edge of the corridor, breathing deeply through his mouth.

This end door was also closed. The lack of a quick exit from the narrow third-floor hallway left him vulnerable. He turned the knob, and his heart leaped as the hinge grated at the first pressure. Carroll froze, his hand on the knob. At first all he could hear was the pounding of his own heart. Hours seemed to drag by as he waited, immobile, his hand cramping with the intensity of his grip. Then, a thrashing sound as someone turned over in bed—and then silence. Carroll persisted, pushing the door open ever wider until he was able to insinuate his body through the opening. Moonlight streamed fully through the windows here at the back of the house, and there she lay. This was, indeed, Gwendolyn MacGowan sleeping before him.

The moonlight lent the room the air of an old gelatin silver print; Gwendolyn's hair was jet-black, streaked with silver, against the white pillow. Carroll ran his left hand slowly up and down over the fabric covering the sheath pressing against his thigh, then gently massaged the knife's satiny wooden handle. Gwendolyn slept on her side, facing away from him.

A gleam on the bookcase next to her bed caught his attention. As he inched closer he caught Gwendolyn's scent—a light mixture of sweat and soap. Carroll reached for the object. It was a frame, containing portraits of two children. He drew in his breath with an audible hiss as he recognized Elinor. He was shaken but replaced the frame soundlessly and backed slowly out of the room, easing the door shut. Despite the shock of the photograph, Carroll felt an incredible lightness. His household was peacefully asleep, and he had earned the right to dine.

CHAPTER TWENTY

"Ready, Eric? It's getting late. I need to get going soon." It was 9:15 Monday morning, and Gwendolyn was anxious to leave, actually looking forward to dropping by her shop, having something other than death to think about—even taxes. She paced around the kitchen and jumped when the phone rang.

"Warren? I tried to get you earlier. I'm glad you called. We're just leaving for the shop. Have you found out anything?"

"Yes, it is me," he laughed. "No, not much we could turn up on a Sunday. He has no police record, and with no license or registration in the DMV computer, our hands are tied. I got men out first thing this morning—they're checking the Department of Social Services in case he's getting welfare, and checking out the post offices in the precincts. Patrol officers are covering the area with the composite and talking to the local postmen. Those guys all know about the characters on their routes."

Gwendolyn looked at the receiver and shivered. "It's beginning to really sink in that he's still out there. I wanted to believe the worst was over, but it's not, is it, until he's found. Have you thought of the BPL?"

"What?"

"The Boston Public Library. If he was so heavily into literary affairs—no pun intended—maybe he has a library card. Or belongs to the Athenaeum."

"I'll get on that—anything that might flush him out is worth a try."

"Just a minute—" Gwendolyn cupped her hand over the receiver. Eric had just walked into the kitchen and was staring vaguely about. "Eric, I want you to go down to the boiler room and bring that bicycle I showed you out to the garage. Use the ramp and wheel it out the side door. I'll go down and lock up after you."

Eric started to protest, but Gwendolyn was in no mood to humor him. "Just do it," she said in a voice that brooked no argument, "whether you want to ride it or not. I'll use it myself. Do you want any breakfast?"

Eric shook his head and disappeared into the cellar. Gwendolyn returned to her conversation.

"That kid's bugging me. I'll be glad when his aunt gets back from her vacation. No, that's not really true. He's got to be going through a lot. I just hate feeling that I'm responsible for whatever's wrong with him …"

"Listen, Gwen, I'll give you a piece of free advice that I had to learn the hard way. A lot of people out there would be happy for you to take up their burdens and responsibilities, and make you feel guilty for every moment they aren't happy. Don't. You didn't cause Eric and his mother to come over here, and you aren't responsible for Monica's death. Eric had plenty wrong with him before he ever set eyes on you, and how he deals with that is up to him. Be there for him; sympathize; be supportive; but that's all you're humanly required to do. That kid would have you playing Mommy to his five-year-old in a minute if he could. Take it from someone who knows."

Gwendolyn was surprised at the intensity of his words but said nothing.

"End of sermon. Don't mind me—I'm on edge too. I'm sure you'll handle the boy just fine."

"No, you're right. Thanks. I'll watch myself. I expect we'll be back around one or two. Would you like me to call you, or would you rather check back here?"

"I'll call you. I'll be in and out, so that'll be easier. You be careful."

They rang off, and Gwendolyn felt better. Of course Eric was upset. It was hard enough to realize that her own mother was dead; how could she expect a kid—anyone—to assimilate his mother's brutal execution in this short time?

Gwendolyn heard Eric pass under the window with the bicycle as Patricia Hanley came in from the living room with her empty coffee mug. "I'll be right up, Pat, I just have to lock the cellar door. Eric is outside with the bike—could you give him a hand putting it in the car?"

"No problem. I've already checked the front door, and the first-floor windows are still latched from last night. We'll be waiting for you in the car."

Carroll sat on the old couch, his knees drawn up to his chest, his eyes bright. He had heard the footsteps descending, listened to the boy struggle as he wheeled the bicycle out the door, saw bicycle wheels and legs pass by the windows. He heard a heavier tread descend and, shortly, ascend again. He'd savored every moment. What an exquisite pleasure to know that it had been in his power to destroy them both in an instant if he had so chosen. Soon.

Cautiously, he unbolted the door in his back room and listened as the car engine started and the wheels crunched down the gravel drive. He waited another half hour before going up to the kitchen.

Searching through the library's *Dun & Bradstreet* volumes on Saturday, Goslin had discovered that Gwendolyn's shop was called The Cambridge Frame, and he knew that to get to that section of North Cambridge, and return, without stopping for any other errands, would take at least an hour and a quarter. If she were going by her store, then, conservatively, she would take at least another half an hour to forty-five minutes. Fixing the bicycle might take another fifteen minutes—or more. He should have a comfortable two to two and a half hours to himself.

Goslin felt the empty house envelop him like a great, vaulted cathedral. No one to account to, no one to hinder him in whatever he chose to do. He took a change of clothes from his bag—fresh boxer shorts, brand-new athletic socks, and navy-blue T-shirt— bundling the shorts and socks into the shirt.

The kitchen was bright with morning sunshine, the scent of buttered toast lingering in the air. Carroll set his bundle down on the table, and went to explore the refrigerator, taking out a single egg and a packet of grated cheese. An untouched place setting—the boy's?—was already laid at the end of the table.

He found clean glasses in the cupboard, poured himself some grapefruit juice and set it by the plate, along with a paper napkin and salt and pepper shakers.

Setting the teapot on to boil, he sought out and assembled the rest of the necessary breakfast ingredients. He whipped up the egg, added shredded cheddar cheese, a dollop of sour cream, thin rings of chopped green onion from a wilting bunch of scallions in the vegetable drawer, and a few dashes each of Tabasco and Worcestershire sauce.

The frying pan, he noticed with distaste, had been left dirty; he scrubbed it out thoroughly and melted a dab of butter before adding his egg mixture and setting it on the flame.

Goslin felt much better after a hot breakfast. He left the pan—dirtied—in the same position in the sink, washed and dried the dish and utensils, and reset the place at the end of the table. He returned the salt and pepper shakers to their spot above the stove, found the waste basket under the sink and threw away the paper napkin, rinsed and dried the juice glass and set it back inside the cupboard, then inspected his handiwork minutely.

"And a fine breakfast it was, too, Mrs. McCarthy," he exclaimed aloud, bowing slightly and laughing at his private childhood joke. In the old days, he would pretend during the Game that his midnight feasts were prepared by his personal housekeeper; an apple-cheeked old-country ancient he'd christened Mary McCarthy. She would do more than fix his meals; she'd lay out his clothes, praise his schoolwork, and, on occasion, tuck him into his narrow bed and sing to him as he fell asleep. When he was young, he knew those songs by heart, but now they had vanished like dust and smoke; like old Mary McCarthy herself.

He was glad she had come to mind again today. It was

appropriate—a pleasant feeling; old Mary here in his house. Carroll hummed as he picked up the roll of clothing and walked toward the front stairs. "No reason to creep up the back way, eh?" he said aloud, taking the main stairs two at a time.

He peeked into each of the two bedrooms he had visited the night before, then entered the three others off this landing. Two led to adjoining, spacious guest rooms. Both had handsome fireplaces bordered in multicolored tiles, topped by heavy oak mantels and ornate mirrors; both had polished tile aprons in front of the hearths. They were larger than the front bedrooms, and most likely had been the master bedroom suite during the old home's heyday.

The remaining door opened into a vast, gleaming bathroom smelling of fresh lemon soap. Small black hexagonal tiles surrounded by small white tiles covered the floor in a dizzying pattern. The walls were done halfway up in gleaming white tile squares, separated by a black tile strip from the glossy, white paint of the upper wall and ceiling. The white glowed against vermillion bath towels on brass rods, each with black washcloths and face towels. One set had been recently used and carelessly replaced, and it was with some effort that he resisted the urge to straighten them.

He flicked on the light switch illuminating a vintage Holophane ribbed glass shade hung from a long brass chain, swagged so that the light shown directly over one end of the white claw-foot tub. A hexagonal white sink was set into a tiled oak cabinet, and either still had, or had been refitted with, an antique brass faucet and handles with white enamel "H" and "C" insets.

"Well, well," he murmured. A more stark and high-tech color combination than he would have chosen to complement the old-fashioned fixtures, but not bad, not bad at all. Mother had always insisted on plain white or beige towels and sheets, day in, day out, year after year. A shame to be so determinedly bland, he had often thought, when there were so many wonderful rich colors in the spectrum. He himself would have chosen navy and maroon and gold, or rust and hunter green and lemon or …

But time was wasting. He adjusted the small bundle under his arm and climbed up to the third floor, sliding his hand along the smooth, cool railing. Gwendolyn's bathroom was also large, with hardwood floors and oak wainscoting instead of tile. To his delight, he saw that Gwendolyn shared his taste for her personal quarters—walls and ceiling were creamy yellow, and there was the mate to the Holophane lamp on the floor below.

Carroll set his shirt roll down on the sink and slipped off his sneakers. He curled his toes in the thick-piled hunter green rug in front of the tub, bent over and put in the plug and turned on a stream of hot water. He walked to the oval window and found he was looking directly down over the end of the driveway and the front half of the garage. All was peaceful. Far down the street, someone was playing rock music, but the loudest sound on Beech Hill was a scolding blue jay on a branch just outside the window.

As Carroll stripped off his clothing, he folded each article and placed it on top of a wicker laundry basket at the end of the tub. He took a deep-gold terrycloth towel and washcloth from a small linen closet next to the sink and set them out on the basket within easy reach.

When the tub was full, he slowly lowered his body into the steaming hot water. A fresh bar of oatmeal soap was pleasingly pebbly against his skin. He rubbed up a thick lather and worked it into his dusty hair, then closed his eyes and soaked. This was all he had ever wanted—some peace. Not to be harried or ridiculed; simply left alone. He wriggled his toes in the warm water, rinsed out his hair under the faucet, then closed his eyes for a few moments before he pulled the plug and watched the bathwater swirl down the drain.

Standing in the empty tub, he dried himself thoroughly with the rough towel, then stepped out onto the mat. Using Gwendolyn's comb, he slicked back his wet hair, then wiped the sink top and tub down thoroughly with the towel. He patted the soap bar dry and placed it back in its copper dish. He looked around carefully for any other marks or discrepancies and then stuffed the towel and washcloth, along with his own dirty clothes, under Gwendolyn's laundry at the bottom of the wicker basket. Carroll paused before closing the lid, breathing lightly. Gwendolyn evidently didn't wear scent or cosmetics. There was an overriding earthy aroma, an impression more of backyard garden than boudoir.

Cool air flowed in from the hallway as Goslin opened the bathroom door. He pulled the door halfway closed, as he had found it, and went directly to Gwendolyn's bedroom. It was quite warm in the room as the sun reached its zenith and beat down on the dark slate roof. In the light of day Carroll was immediately aware of the piles of papers and letters, and he sank to his knees in front of the stacks.

He picked one up and was rent with such hatred and yearning that it took his breath. He swayed, his vision darkening so that, for a moment, he was unable to discern the writing on the paper. He dropped it as though it had scorched his fingers. There was no need in any case to torment himself reading it over. Every word, written or received, was already engraved upon his mind and heart. Perhaps that, he thought, was his sickness and his curse—never to forget, never to be able to put the past behind him.

Then, as he stood up, he saw the manuscript at the foot of the bed. He moved closer but did not touch it.

He was walking downtown with Father. Years ago, now it was, before Father had left. He remembered the day with great clarity. They were passing a vacant lot when Carroll noticed a sign stating, *Owner Will Build to Suit Tenant*. He'd asked what that meant, "to suit tenant," and then, after Father explained, he had puzzled for weeks over the disturbing implications of such a promise. How could the owner predict what might "suit" a prospective tenant? How much could one demand? Would the owner then have to build *anything*? What if someone demanded a pyramid? A castle? It seemed a terribly risky offer.

Yet hadn't he offered exactly that to Elinor? A veritable vacant soul, upon which she was able to demand that he build anything and everything that suited her fancy? And he had tried. But after the ribbons were cut and the cornerstone laid, Elinor lost interest, abandoning the ramshackle structure he had undertaken, leaving him in sole possession of this squalid tenement of self. What most surprised him now, was how very long it had taken for the scales to fall from his eyes.

Elinor had certainly known what he was going to ask as she sat there waiting, watching not him, but her manuscript in his hands.

"I'm all alone now," he'd begun, "and *you're* all alone—I mean, with Gwendolyn way out … *there*—and I was thinking, I mean I still feel, that is, it would be an honor if you …"

She rose quickly, fanning herself with her hand, though it was quite cool in the curtained room. "I don't know what's the matter with me—I've come over all headachy. I need to lie down. You go now—we'll talk after you've read the book, Carroll. You're such a dear."

As soon as he'd stood up, Elinor seemed to regain her strength and took charge, making sure he had the xerox carton, hustling him to the elevator, then out the basement door with a quick peck on his cheek, giving him no time to protest.

Out on the sidewalk Goslin adjusted the carton under his arm and, putting aside Elinor's peremptory good-bye, began to think of the future. This fall, and on into the winter months, they would sit in the newly decorated living room, a fire crackling in the great marble fireplace, working—*together*—on their novel. Whether or not Elinor would ever admit it to herself, they both knew that he, Carroll, had been the instrument of *The Ceremony of Innocence*'s success. He would be her mentor again and forge the triumph of her second novel.

It was far too nice an evening to go directly home. He hadn't spent much time outdoors in … oh, ages. He decided to start in on the manuscript right here, in the warm, open air. He walked across to the Gardens and sat down on a bench in view of the Swan Boats. He leaned back against the bench and pulled open the box and began to read *The Lying Days of Youth*.

Now the daughter knew it all. And who else? How many others had looked at it, read it, laughed at it—and at him? His rage drained, replaced with calm acceptance. No, there was to be no peace, but there could be justice. He would never see Mother's house again, but it never would be—never had been—a place of sanctuary, of love or peace. Today; tomorrow; ten years from now; Mother's bird-watchers or whoever would inherit the place. It no longer mattered to him. He laughed a little at the thought, realizing that indifference was the key to the Game. Mother, Elinor; they had pinned all their hopes on his caring, and without that, why, Mrs. McCarthy was more real than either one of them.

Goslin looked at the paper on the floor, the years sifting in yellowing heaps around his ankles. He was relieved that there was very little left to play out; that peace might lie simply in seeing the final chapter of the farce he called his life through to the end.

The phone rang, breaking into his thoughts. He counted the rings ... nineteen, twenty, twenty-one ... Someone had something important to communicate. As the ringing went on and on, Goslin looked around the room very carefully. When it finally stopped, he picked up the phone and pushed the ringer toggle to "Off." He had fixed in his mind the position of the bookcase with the photo of little Elinor, the bedside table, the white iron bed. He hesitated a moment, then went back and turned the phone switch to "On." As he closed the door and started downstairs, the ringing began again.

"Who wants some lunch?" asked Gwendolyn as they trooped through the back door. "Cold chicken and potato salad with iced tea or Coke. Eric? Pat?"

"Sounds good. Tea for me, please. I'll help set the table."

Eric didn't say anything, but he opened the refrigerator door and took out the platter of chicken and the jug of iced tea.

Gwendolyn pulled off the tinfoil and took a second look at the plate. "Somebody get hungry in the night? I thought we had more left over than this."

"Nope, not me," said Patricia, "I dropped right off and slept like a log."

Eric shook his head.

"That's odd. Maybe …" Gwendolyn began, then stopped short as the phone rang.

"Good timing. We just came in a few minutes ago. Have you found him?"

"No," said Thibodeau, "and I've been calling you every few minutes for the last hour. I tried to catch you at your shop, but you had just left. What took you so long?" He sounded both anxious and irritated.

"Remember? We took the bike with us. We had to go to four different gas stations before we found one with a working air pump …"

"Well, forget about the bike for now, Gwen. We found out where Goslin lives. You were right, by the way, about the library card. That's the only thing we turned up in his own name."

"Terrific," cried Gwendolyn. "Did you find out anything at his house?"

"We haven't gone in yet. We've filed the affidavits for a search warrant, but that will take two hours, minimum, and I'm pretty sure we won't find him at home anyway. There's no car behind his building, so if we've got the right man, he's on the prowl somewhere. I put out an APB, and have officers on foot going over your area street by street, and I'm beefing up the patrol cars.

I've got to stay down here for a while, but I'll be checking in. I'll try to get over there later."

"We'll be right here. Call when you can."

"Remember, Gwen, he's armed. I want all of you to stay inside until further notice. Watch TV, play cards, whatever. But don't linger near the windows and don't go outside—you'd be sitting ducks on the patio."

Goslin shifted uncomfortably in the cramped dumbwaiter shaft that opened behind the old couch. The small doorway in the basement slid open easily, and he found that if he worked his way into the space, he could stand upright with his head just above the level of the kitchen floor. From that vantage point, he could overhear most of the conversation in the room through the cabinets along the rear kitchen wall.

What he had just heard was disquieting. They were looking for him, had located the house, perhaps even knew his name, or had found the car. In any case, the circle was closing. But this time he wouldn't be pushed. Tension was building in the house; he could feel it wrapping about him, tightening. It was inevitable that they would check down here; if not this afternoon, surely tonight. He couldn't stay in his room as he had planned. Even now he could feel them intruding, snooping through his room, searching the basement, window by window, door by door.

First he would replace the basement window, then make his way to the second floor. If he could reach one of those empty rooms, he should be safe for as long as he needed. It was unlikely that they would do more than glance in or check the windows, at most. If he remained alert, the connecting door between the two upstairs bedrooms would give him the latitude to move, should they decide to check the whole house. The second floor would give him more freedom, to go either up or downstairs. He couldn't tamper with the phones this early, but he would be sure they were disconnected tonight.

He heard the scrape and clatter of dishes being cleared as he emerged gingerly from the dumbwaiter. He stowed his gear in the duffel bag, slung the strap over his shoulder so that the bag hung directly down behind his back, and inched up the back stairs.

"I want you two to stay here in the living room," said Patricia. "I'm going to secure the garage and make sure the cars are locked up. There won't be any bike riding today, Eric." Eric smiled in relief, although he almost preferred to risk the bicycle rather than be closeted with Gwendolyn.

The movies that had previously been such a pleasure for them all became a chore once they were confined. By five thirty they had watched four episodes of *The Rockford Files* and were bored to death with one another's company. There had been no word from Thibodeau; they were tensed, waiting for the phone to ring.

"I'm going out to fix us something for dinner," said Gwendolyn in desperation. "Maybe Mexican. I have some frozen hamburger, and it won't take long to heat. I've got a few onions and cans of the rest of the stuff."

Gwendolyn felt a vast relief as she escaped to the solitude of the kitchen. It seemed far-fetched to be getting cabin fever after four hours, but she felt as if she had been snowbound on K2 for months. She leaped at the phone's ring and snatched it up. "Warren!"

"Sorry for the delay—it took forever to get the search warrant through. I mean, the guy's killed two people, and they still put stumbling blocks in our way. Anyway, we got into the house. Nobody there, of course, but we found the room and the portrait that Eric described. We found that Bible—that told us that the mother's maiden name was Tallmadge. The reason we had so much trouble was that the house and the car, the phone and so forth, were all kept in her name. Now that we have her registration, we'll find the car if it's in the area."

"Can you come over?" Gwendolyn didn't realize how eager she was for Warren's company until she heard him answer in the negative.

"I'd like to, but I have to keep things going here. Goslin can't be far away. We've got his house covered now, and we'll be keeping close tabs on your place. You're staying in, aren't you?"

"Yes. Pat went out just after you called and locked up the cars and the garage, but we've been sitting in the living room since then. I'm in the kitchen now, about to make up one of my terrific Mexican dinners. Sure you can't join us?" Gwendolyn was horrified at the girlish, wheedling tone she heard in her voice, and rushed on before Thibodeau could answer. "No, don't mind me, Warren. I didn't mean to pressure you. Go on with whatever you've got to do."

"I'll be calling back. I've beefed up the patrol cars, and I've got men walking the beat in the area. Just hang in there and do whatever Pat Hanley says. And make sure that Eric doesn't wander off."

"He's been pretty docile. Still too quiet, if you ask me, but I haven't been beating myself over it, thanks to your advice. Besides—there are more important things to worry about. You take care—we'll be here by the phone."

The spicy smell of salsa wafted up to the second floor and made Goslin salivate. He didn't particularly care for Mexican, but suddenly his stomach was crying out for food. He forced his mind away from the idea of eating. He had had a good breakfast, and it wouldn't do to weaken now. By keeping the door to the bedroom open about eighteen inches, he could clearly determine where the others were and what they were doing. The thick doors were effective sound barriers, but the long, polished hallways were amplifiers. If he remained alert, he would hear anyone coming up the stairs and would be able to ease the door shut in time.

These rooms were even better situated for his purposes. He could see the driveway and the front of the garage from the windows, and he had easy access to the other bedrooms. He was light and free again. His bag was hidden under the darkest recess of the big double bed, and the gun and bowie knife lay ready on the coverlet.

The sun was low in the sky, the air still muggy, when the three finished supper. The big house was closing in now that they didn't have the option of walking about outdoors or sitting on the patio, and they were all restless and irritable.

Pat Hanley shrugged out of her short-sleeved cotton overshirt, exposing the .38 on her hip. "I should have checked the cellar last night and didn't, so I want to make sure I get it done before dark tonight."

"Do you want us to come too?" asked Gwendolyn.

"Not necessary," Pat replied, touching her sidearm. "You two just finish up here or go on into the living room. I'll be back directly."

"Everything okay?" Gwendolyn looked up as Patricia came back into the living room. She was attempting to work on some of the tax material she had brought home from the shop, but she couldn't concentrate. The figures danced in a meaningless jumble before her eyes, and she finally pushed the papers away in frustration.

"All the windows are latched and the doors locked. I'm afraid we'll just have to sweat it out. But Thibodeau's good. He's got a reputation downtown as a real stickler for detail. I think he'll get the guy as quickly as it can be done. We'll just dig in and wait. Do you have any cards or games?"

"I think I've got an old Monopoly set upstairs," said Gwendolyn.

"That would kill some time. I haven't played that since I was a kid."

"I'll run up and get it."

Gwendolyn wasn't aware exactly how jumpy she was until she began to climb the long, dimly lit stairway to her bedroom.

The farther away she got from the living room, the spookier she felt. She stopped on the first landing and looked down the hall. Everything was quiet, the doors shut, the only sound the pad of her rubber-soled shoes.

The high vault of the ceiling arched over her, the angles of the stairs and landing cast masses of shadow above her head, and the light from the frosted bulbs gleamed on the polished wood, while the balusters threw bars of shadow across the walls. The air grew hotter and closer as she reached the third floor. Even up here, she could hear Pat and Eric talking in the living room, almost clearly enough to distinguish their words.

Gwendolyn was surprised to see how dark it had gotten when she opened her bedroom door. She switched on the light, and after a short bit of rummaging about in her closet, found the game. Before turning off the overhead light, Gwendolyn turned on the reading lamp by her bed and switched on the little fan. She breathed easier with each step that brought her closer to her companions.

CHAPTER TWENTY-ONE

"This sucks, Ed." Thibodeau drummed his fingers on the steering wheel and glanced over at Albano. "Can I bum a cigarette?"

"Not on your life. The last time you mooched one, you smoked it, then chewed me out for letting you have it. What's eating you, anyway?"

"For all we've got on this Goslin, he's still out there, armed and deranged."

Thibodeau and Albano were patrolling the side streets of Jamaica Plain, but so far had seen neither a man fitting Goslin's description nor any trace of his car. A bartender on the evening shift at the Galway House had identified the photo, remarking that he was "not one of the regulars," remembering only that Goslin had had difficulty deciding on a brand of beer and opted instead for "a draft." The barman couldn't remember anything unusual about his clothing—"Something dark, I think, but everything looks dark in here"—or whether he had been carrying anything.

"Let's try the other side of the pond," said Thibodeau, swinging down toward the Jamaicaway. They drove for a while through a residential area, when suddenly Albano cried, "Bingo!" A green Volvo with the Tallmadge plates was parked in front of a brick house. "Call in and get a team over here to dust and impound it."

The elderly couple who lived in the brick house were accommodating but uninformative. Yes, they had noticed the car when they returned home yesterday evening, but they had assumed it belonged to a neighbor's guest. They had never seen the car before, nor did they know anyone who resembled the composite photo.

Two patrol cars had arrived by the time the detectives finished questioning the couple. Thibodeau set two men to attend to the car, and another pair to canvass the neighborhood with photographs, then set off again with Albano.

"I like it less and less," Thibodeau muttered. "That means he's been out on foot since last night."

"Or, he could have ditched the car here as a ploy," suggested Albano. "He could be in LA or—anywhere."

"I don't buy that. He didn't need a ploy. With over twenty-four-hours' head start, he could have just left the car at home and taken the T to the airport."

"Well, how about a tease to make us think he is around? No, that doesn't figure either. If he wanted to lead us on, he'd have put it nearer her house, not this far away."

"Mmmm." Thibodeau frowned and drove in silence. He pulled into the Dunkin' Donuts near the corner of Centre and Greenough. "Go in and get some coffee and donuts, will you, pal? I want to make a phone call."

Thibodeau dropped a dime in the slot and was relieved to hear Gwendolyn's "Hello?"

"We found the car," he said. "On a side street on the far side of the pond. Won't tell us much, I suspect. But now he doesn't have a place to go back to or a car to go there in. How're you folks doing?"

"Well," Gwendolyn laughed, "we've been teaching Eric how to play Monopoly, and I think the greedy little slumlord is going to bankrupt us both. We're fine, though, just suffering from a surfeit of popcorn and each other's company. Pat went downstairs after dinner and checked out the cellar. Everything's locked up tight. How about you?"

"Ed and I are down at the Dunkin' Donuts getting something to eat. You keep playing Monopoly. We've got a lot of men on this, Gwen, and Ed and I are going to be out looking, too. And speak of the Devil, here he comes now."

"You've cleaned me out," grumbled Pat Hanley, throwing up her hands in mock surrender.

"Yep. I'm just a pauper again," sighed Gwendolyn, "Me, who once had a hotel on Boardwalk and Park Place."

Eric grinned, counting his stacks of colored money. "That was fun."

"I enjoyed it, too," said Gwendolyn, smiling and reaching out tentatively to tousle the boy's lank hair. He didn't flinch as she feared he might but smiled back.

Eric got up slowly and stretched. "I'm tired."

Gwendolyn glanced at the clock on the VCR. "No wonder. It's after eleven. I'm going to get my glass of ice water and go on up to bed. Anybody want anything in the kitchen?"

"No thanks," said Pat Hanley. "I'll recheck the first-floor doors and windows and then we should be all set. By the way, is there a lock on the door to the basement?"

Gwendolyn thought a moment. "Not the one at the top of the stairs, but there's a bolt on the one at the bottom."

"I'll bolt that too. No use taking any chances. The windows are all locked, but you can't hear very well in here with the doors closed."

"We'll wait for you and then we can all go up together." Gwendolyn rinsed out her big glass and packed it full of ice cubes. Pat came up from the cellar and eyed her quizzically.

"One of my little oddities. I love ice water, and I found these big glasses that hold about a quart. Want some? I'll fix you one."

"Thanks. I guess I'm thirsty after all—the heat and the popcorn. I'll probably have to go to the bathroom half a dozen times, but what the hell."

After Pat had closed and locked the first-floor windows and checked the front and back doors, they filed upstairs with Gwendolyn in the lead. After Eric and Pat said good night and went into their rooms, Gwendolyn started alone up to the third floor, very glad that she had left a light burning in her room.

Goslin lay in the dark, the full moon rising above the beech trees, its light spilling in through the windows, pale as his motionless face. He had heard the good nights just steps away from his door and listened to Gwendolyn's footsteps pass down the hallway above him. Now all was silent.

He lay perfectly still, his breathing slow and steady, hands folded on his chest and a smile curving the corners of his thin lips. He was fully dressed and ready. His knife and pistol lay on the bed to his right. After estimating that a half hour had passed, Goslin eased himself off the bed and glided noiselessly to the door. He opened it the merest crack so that he would hear anyone moving about, then retreated to the bed and waited another thirty minutes.

He switched on the red-lensed penlight and searched through the duffel bag, laying out the items he would need to bring with him. He attached one end of a roll of two-inch-wide surgical tape to the bed frame and unrolled it slowly to muffle the noise. He cut an eighteen-inch length with the penknife and stuck it to the left shoulder of his jacket, and another small square, with which he taped the handcuff key to the back of his left hand. He wrapped the penknife in a handkerchief and put it into his left jacket pocket along with an opened set of handcuffs, putting the second pair of opened cuffs in his right pocket.

He hooked the sheathed bowie knife inside his waistband, flat against his left leg, checked the loaded clip in the Savage, and tucked the pistol into his right pants pocket. He walked about the room, testing the weight and balance of the various objects. The pistol was a tight fit, but it held as he walked and sat reasonably well as he moved. He took a deep breath and stood upright, listening at the door. The house was silent. It was time.

Drinking their lukewarm coffee, Thibodeau and Albano sat in the car a hundred yards down the street from Gwendolyn's driveway. From their vantage point, they were not conspicuous to any passersby, but commanded a view both up the side street on the garage end of the house, and of the driveway itself.

"Lights out upstairs now," commented Thibodeau. "I hope they can get some sleep."

"Well, there haven't been any signs of the guy being around today," said Albano.

"I know, I know. But something doesn't sit right."

"There's a full moon, Warren. We've got a good chance of seeing anyone who moves in."

"Only from these two sides … There goes the black-and-white. At least those boys are on their toes." Thibodeau sucked moodily on his coffee and hunched down into the seat.

Goslin's adrenaline was flowing as he set out. He yearned to rush into each sleeper's room swinging the great knife, finishing them all in a fine frenzy. It had taken all his control this morning not to throw himself on the boy and Gwendolyn as they walked smugly past his door.

He paused on the second-floor landing, hand on the banister, waiting for his breathing to steady before going on. He was grateful that Gwendolyn had chosen the back of the house for her suite. It was not directly over the other bedrooms where the others might hear footsteps or other noises.

As he approached, Goslin saw that the door was closed. Remembering that it had resisted the night before, he grasped the knob firmly, inching it around until it released soundlessly.

Gwendolyn was in the first, deep stages sleep, after having lain awake for nearly an hour. She was facing Carroll, left arm outflung, right arm thrown crooked under the covers, her face a ghostly mask in the bluish light. His footsteps muffled by the whirr of the small fan, Goslin moved closer to the bed, step by measured step, until he was a scant yard from Gwendolyn's motionless form. He reached into his right pocket and by imperceptible degrees drew out the cuffs.

Despite his caution, the chain made a tiny chink as it pulled free. Gwendolyn made a small questioning noise, and Goslin instantly launched himself across her body, pinning her arm and snapping the cuff shut on her left wrist. Gwendolyn bolted fully awake and opened her mouth to scream, but Goslin, now holding her arm outstretched by the cuff chain, clamped his free hand over her mouth. He stretched her arm back to the white iron bars of the bedstead and hooked the free cuff around it and clicked it shut.

With Goslin's full weight bearing down on her, Gwendolyn couldn't free her right arm, nor could she kick with her legs confined by the covers. Goslin stripped the piece of tape off his shoulder and slapped it over her mouth, pulling her forward to wrap the tape tightly behind her head. He ignored the muffled noises issuing deep within her throat; however loud they sounded to him, he knew they wouldn't be heard downstairs.

Making sure the tape was secure, Goslin pulled himself up astride her writhing form, unmindful that the leather sheath had worked around to the inside of his thigh and was digging painfully into her stomach. He grasped her free right hand, then pulled the second pair of handcuffs out of his left pocket. He secured her right wrist, then, hitching up so his knees were nearly under her armpits, he reached the cuff around one of the iron bars and secured the loose end to her already fettered left hand. Satisfied that she was sufficiently silenced and immobilized, he peeled the tape off the back of his hand, retrieved the key, and unlocked the first cuff.

He got up off the bed, checked to see that his gun and knife were secure, then put the freed pair of cuffs back in his pocket. "Don't go away, Mrs. MacGowan. I'll be right back."

"Stay here, Ed. I'm going to check out the house. Where's the flashlight?"

"Here. Be careful, man."

"I've got to take a leak, anyway—coffee does a number on me. They ought to have a head in these heaps."

Monday night was quiet; none of the weekend party noise, no blaring music, not even a walker out with his dog. The heat had sapped everyone's energy. Thibodeau moved up the driveway, the moonlight showing the way.

The driveway and yard were clearly visible, but the dark hedge all around the house would offer ample cover. Thibodeau stepped behind the leafy barrier and relieved himself against the wall. Reaching the house, he switched on the flashlight, examining each basement window. He crossed the open patio with his light off, and gently tested the back and cellar doors. The big side door was locked tight. He moved on, shining his light down into the open front basement room where he had talked with Gwendolyn and Eric. He was rounding the front of the house when something stopped him. Thibodeau turned back and shone his light on the corner window. He parted the bushes and stepped in for a closer look. At a certain angle, the beam caught a thin, etched line running completely around the edge of one pane. Thibodeau knelt down and gently nudged the center of the glass. It gave, then slewed sideways and fell onto the basement floor with an audible crash. "Shit!" He dropped the flashlight and ran for the front door as he unsnapped his holster.

It never fails, thought Pat Hanley. I've known since I was six that I shouldn't drink anything before I go to bed. She pulled on her robe and slippers and slipped her .38 into her pocket. She opened her bedroom door—and looked into the face of Carroll Goslin.

Goslin had barely reached the bottom of the stairs on the second floor when he heard a noise in the first bedroom. He had just time to pull the Savage out of his pocket when the door opened, and the red-haired woman nearly walked into him.

As she fumbled in her bathrobe pocket, Goslin raised his gun without aiming, simply pointing his finger, and fired twice. The woman cried out and fell to the floor, moaning.

Goslin wrenched open the second door and burst in on Eric, who had only time to open his eyes before the man strode to the bed and hauled him out by the arm.

"Put your hands behind you," Goslin ordered. Eric did as he was told, and Goslin clamped the cuffs on him, securing them as tightly as possible on the boy's thin wrists. He yanked up on the chain, eliciting a cry of pain. "Upstairs," Goslin commanded, and Eric, whimpering, stumbled on ahead of him.

"Call for backup, and follow me in," Thibodeau panted into his walkie-talkie to Albano. "Something's going down in there." As Thibodeau fumbled in his wallet for Gwendolyn's key, he heard two shots.

Goslin prodded Eric into the bedroom ahead of him, shoving him across the piles of papers and down onto the heap of clothes on the lounge chair by the window. Gwendolyn rolled her eyes wildly as Eric tripped through the door. She had heard the shots downstairs and assumed there would be no help from Patricia Hanley.

He put the pistol back in his pocket and leaned over Gwendolyn. In her thrashing she had kicked the covers off the bed, and, as Goslin bent closer, she pivoted on her hip and swung her feet into his midriff. He lurched sideways into the bedside table, tipping over the glass. Ice water soaked Goslin's pants as the glass fell and smashed on the hardwood floor. Goslin swore and kicked at the fragments.

"You bitch," he hissed. Gwendolyn pulled away from him as far as she could as he drew the knife from its sheath.

Eric felt faint as he saw the flash of the deadly blade. He knew the man would kill them both this time. Eric twisted his wrists, yanking and pulling, gasping at the searing pain as the metal cuffs bit into his wrists, opening the old wounds. He felt the hot, slick blood pouring out. He forced himself to slow down, He held his right hand steady and rotated the left, and this time, lubricated by his own blood, his left wrist popped free of the cuff. He kept his hands behind him, groping desperately about him for anything at all, when suddenly, among the strewn clothing, his hand closed on something hard.

"It's 'Scott,' Elinor." Goslin bent over Gwendolyn, turning her head toward him with his free hand. "The weakling who crawled away from you in Atlanta—who knuckled under to your husband and left with his tail between his legs. Do you still despise me? I loved you, Elinor, but you ruined it all." Goslin began to cry, great racking sobs, his long fingers caressing the blade.

He caught his breath. "You're going to die, Elinor, but first you *must* understand how wrong you were. How cruel. You can see that now, can't you? You *do* understand?"

He laid the flat of the blade across Gwendolyn's collarbones, pressing just hard enough to draw a thin line of blood. Gwendolyn lay still as death and stared into Goslin's eyes.

"Don't …" Eric's fingers identified the outline of the small revolver Gwendolyn carried in her watch pocket. He worked it free, fitting the small butt into his right hand.

Goslin straightened up slowly and turned to face him. Eric, still seated, the loose handcuff swinging from his wrist, raised the revolver and pointed it at the man. As Goslin moved toward him, Eric pulled the trigger. Nothing.

Thibodeau drew and cocked his revolver as he entered the house. There was no one in the downstairs hall, but he saw lights on upstairs. Hugging the wall he raced up the stairs. Pat Hanley lay unmoving before him. Thibodeau knelt over her, feeling her throat for a pulse. At the touch of his hand she managed to whisper, "Upstairs …"

Thibodeau radioed again to Albano. "Officer down—second floor. Ambulance! Bad situation on the third. Going up."

"Hang in there, Pat." He moved on.

What was wrong? Eric squeezed the trigger again, and nothing happened. He noticed the hammer, thumbed it back and let it snap forward. There was a sharp crack and Goslin staggered back in surprise, dropped the knife, and clutched at his right shoulder. Not taking his eyes off Eric, Goslin bent his knees, lowering his body until he could reach the knife with his left hand. He grasped the handle and straightened slowly, then moved inexorably toward Eric.

Gwendolyn had rolled as far over onto her left side as she could and now kicked out at anything she could reach to distract Goslin. With a strength born of terror, she lashed out at the bedside table that fell against the bookshelf. The fan and telephone flew off the table and the framed photographs fell off the shelf and smashed on the floor. The drawer opened, and the Steyr spilled out, thudding and sliding uselessly under the bed. Momentarily distracted, Goslin glanced back and then turned again to Eric.

As quickly as he could manipulate the hammer, Eric thumbed it back and released—three times—missing first as he swung his hand in a wild arc, then twice more, hitting Goslin in the chest and stomach, but he stumbled on.

"No!" Eric threw the little pistol at the looming white face and slumped to the floor.

The man leaned over him, coughing, blood bubbling from his lips. A drop splashed on Eric's cheek. He scrabbled across a tide of papers, wincing as he put his hand down on a sliver of broken glass.

The man reached down, grabbing Eric by the collar of his pajamas. Eric began to scream hysterically and snatched up the jagged base of the broken water glass, flailing upward, driving a long shard deeply under the man's jaw. Hot blood sprayed over Eric's face and in his eyes, blinding him. The man's grip loosened, and Eric fell back on the floor, sobbing.

Thibodeau appeared in the doorway, sweeping the room with his revolver, but the drama was over. He cautiously approached Goslin, whose gasps were subsiding. "Elinor …" he whispered. The breathing stopped.

Eric struggled to crawl toward the bed. "Gwendolyn," he sobbed, "are you all right?" Thibodeau helped him up. "Take it easy, son, take it easy." He sat the boy on the edge of the bed and then turned to Gwendolyn. He peeled the tape from her mouth as gently as he could.

"Warren …"

"Don't try to talk. I'll get those cuffs off. You'll be all right now, Gwen. You'll both be all right."

CHAPTER TWENTY-TWO

"Yes, my father was your father too, Eric." Gwendolyn groped for the right words. It was Wednesday evening, and they were sitting in Thibodeau's living room. "I'm sorry you had to find out the way you did."

Eric had been sedated Monday night and spent all Tuesday in bed, nearly hysterical when he first woke, calming as the day wore on. Gwendolyn hovered by his bed and waited on him, bringing ginger ale and sherbet, until Eric finally shooed her away and slept soundly for several hours. Towards evening, he showered and dressed and came down to the living room to sit companionably by Gwendolyn as they watched *The Philadelphia Story*.

When Thibodeau had called earlier this afternoon with the news that Pat Hanley was out of intensive care, and invited the two them over for a little celebration, both Gwendolyn and Eric jumped at the opportunity.

"It was a shock to me as well, to learn about you," continued Gwendolyn, smiling at the boy. "Ten days ago I didn't even know you existed, and now you've saved my life."

"I saved your life?"

"You certainly did," said Thibodeau. "Goslin was just about to use that knife when you distracted him—then managed to fire that little pistol. I would have been too late."

"I was so afraid," whispered Eric. "I don't remember doing anything."

"What's important is that you did," said Gwendolyn. "I was terrified too. I can still feel that blade on my skin."

"Well, Goslin is history now, poor bastard," said Thibodeau. "By the way, Eric, we searched for your watch. It wasn't in the back of Goslin's car, or anywhere in the alley. If you lost it there, it was long gone by morning. I know it meant a lot to you, and I'm sorry."

Eric looked at his freshly bandaged wrists. "That's OK, Mr. Thibodeau ...I found out it wasn't what I thought it was. I'll get a new one."

Gwendolyn and Thibodeau exchanged glances, but kept silent.

After a few moments, Thibodeau cleared his throat. "Let's talk about pleasant things for the rest of the evening. Eric, what are your plans now?"

Pleased at being addressed directly rather than discussed, Eric grinned. "Gwendolyn and I have been talking, Mr. Thibodeau, and I'm thinking I'll need to go back to England and live with my aunt ..."

"*I'm* hoping he'll stay here a few weeks more-maybe a while longer ..." Gwendolyn started to stammer, "while we make plans, I mean, no need to rush off now that I've just found you ... met you ..."

"My aunt won't be back for a bit, anyway, and I don't yet know what *she'll* want. We didn't see her often ... But I'll need to find something I can do for a living. I've always liked math and figures … maybe I'll take courses in accounting. It's scary to think of being on my own, though," he added, a trace of uncertainty creeping back.

"You'll do just fine," Thibodeau assured him. "In fact, you sound like a lad who's gone beyond wanting the bicycle I was going to get you. I was talking to a pal down at the station this morning who owes me a few favors. He's going to lend me his kid's moped. Since you're going to be around a few more days, I'll bring it over tomorrow afternoon, and you can try it out. What do you say?"

Eric gulped, then beamed. "I'd like that, Mr. Thibodeau. I may as well fall off something with a motor. If I'm going to fall off—and maybe I won't."

"Sounds like it's going to be a busy day," said Gwendolyn, standing up. "We'd all better get some rest." She turned to Thibodeau and gave him a quick hug. Stepping back, she held out her hand to Eric and then put her arm around his shoulder. "Come on, little brother, let's go home."

CPSIA information can be obtained at www.ICGtesting.com
Printed in the USA
BVOW042104201112

306100BV00001B/2/P